For Corina Isabel Villena-Aldama
—Frederick Luis Aldama

For Dylan, Abigale, James, and MJ
—Oscar Garza

For all those forced from homes and homelands
—Frederick and Oscar

For Corina Isabel Villena-Aldama
—Frederick Luis Aldama

For Dylan, Abigale, James, and MJ
—Oscar Garza

For all those forced from homes and homelands
—Frederick and Oscar

THROUGH FENCES

THROUGH FENCES

Written by Frederick Luis Aldama

Illustrated by Oscar Garza

Edited by Rolando Esquivel

MAD CREEK BOOKS, AN IMPRINT OF
THE OHIO STATE UNIVERSITY PRESS
COLUMBUS

Mad Creek Books, an imprint of The Ohio State University Press.

Library of Congress Cataloging-in-Publication Data
Names: Aldama, Frederick Luis, 1969– author. | Garza, Oscar (Comic book artist
    and writer), illustrator.
Title: Through fences / written by Frederick Luis Aldama ; illustrated by Oscar
    Garza.
Other titles: Latinographix: The Ohio State Latinx comics series. Description:
    Columbus : Mad Creek Books, an imprint of The Ohio State University
    Press, [2024] | Series: Latinographix | Audience: Grades 10–12 | Summary:
    "Collection of short comics about life near the US-Mexico border. Touches
    on issues of immigration, detainment, policing, sexuality, racism, and vio-
    lence"—Provided by publisher.
Identifiers: LCCN 2023031777 | ISBN 9780814258958 (paperback) | ISBN
    0814258956 (paperback) | ISBN 9780814283240 (ebook) | ISBN
    0814283241 (ebook)
Subjects: LCSH: Hispanic American children—Mexican-American Border
    Region—Comic books, strips, etc. | Hispanic American young adults—
    Mexican-American Border Region—Comic books, strips, etc. | Mexican-
    American Border Region—Social conditions—Comic books, strips, etc. |
    Mexican-American Border Region—Social life and customs—Comic books,
    strips, etc. | Mexico—Emigration and immigration—Comic books, strips, etc.
    | CYAC: Graphic novels—Fiction. | Hispanic Americans—Fiction. | Immigra-
    tion—Fiction. | Mexican-American Border Region—Fiction. | LCGFT: Short
    stories. | Graphic novels.
Classification: LCC PZ7.7.A3526 Th 2024 | DDC 741.5/973—dc23/eng/20230809
LC record available at https://lccn.loc.gov/2023031777

Cover illustration by Oscar Garza
Cover design by Charles Brock

PRINTED IN CHINA

♾ The paper used in this publication meets the minimum requirements of the
American National Standard for Information Sciences—Permanence of Paper
for Printed Library Materials. ANSI Z39.48-1992.

CONTENTS

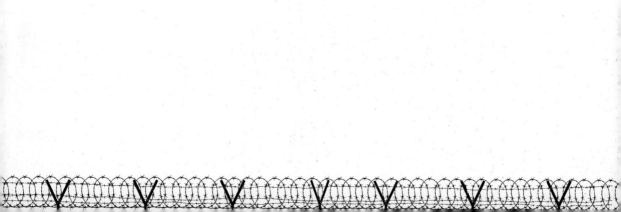

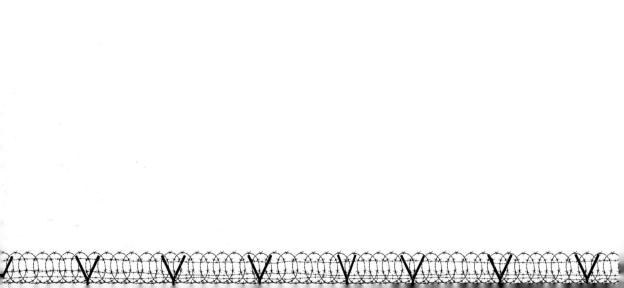

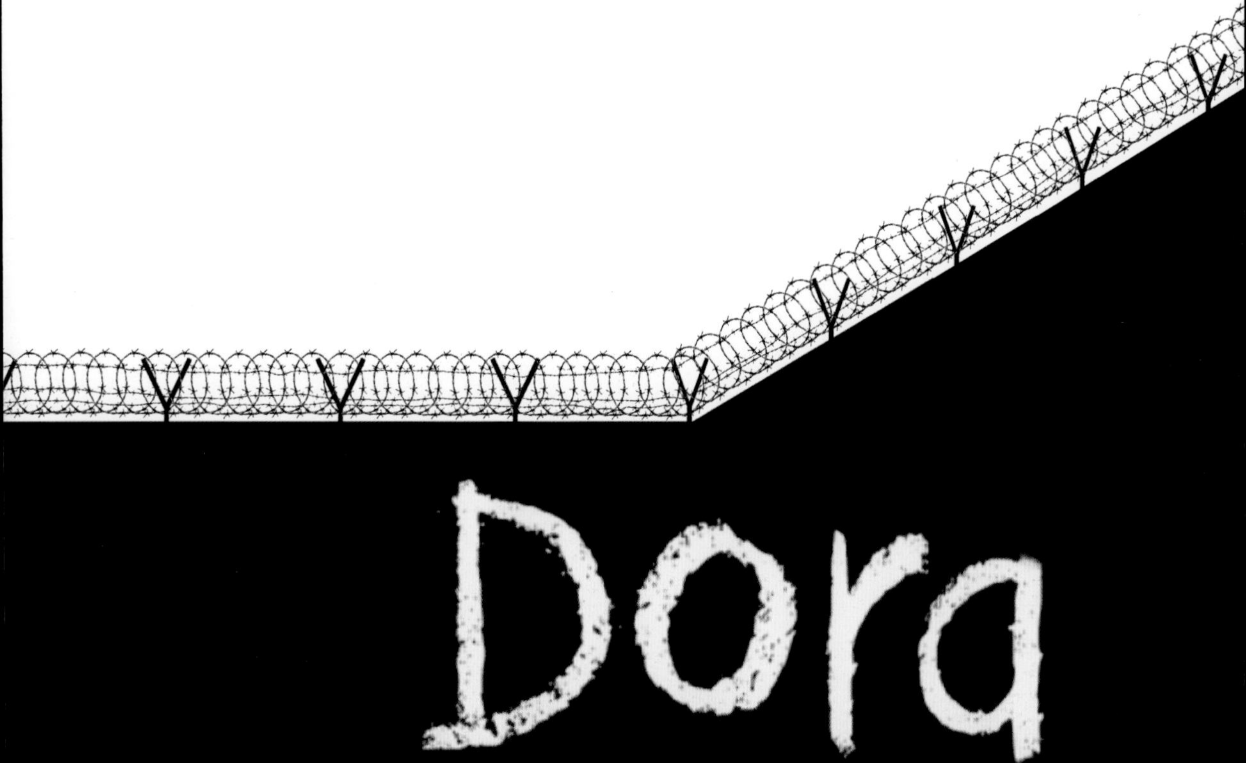
Dora

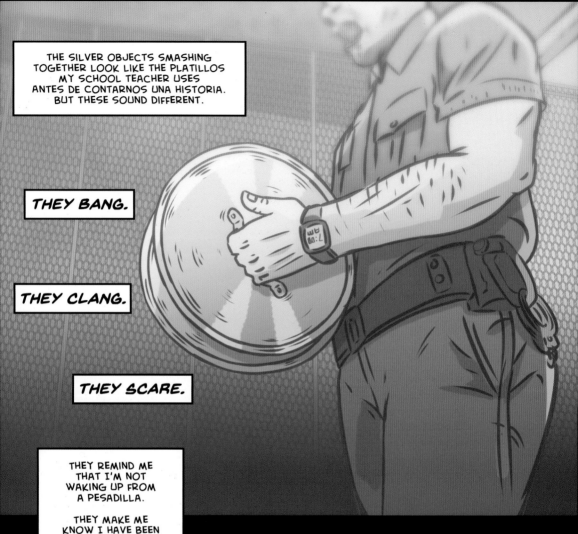

THE SILVER OBJECTS SMASHING TOGETHER LOOK LIKE THE PLATILLOS MY SCHOOL TEACHER USES ANTES DE CONTARNOS UNA HISTORIA. BUT THESE SOUND DIFFERENT.

THEY BANG.

THEY CLANG.

THEY SCARE.

THEY REMIND ME THAT I'M NOT WAKING UP FROM A PESADILLA.

THEY MAKE ME KNOW I HAVE BEEN LEJOS DE CASA FOR QUITE SOME TIME.

I JOLT UPRIGHT. YA ES HORA DE LEVANTARME. I RUB MY STICKY EYES. I SEE THE BIG PEOPLE IN GREEN WALKING UP AND DOWN THE ROW OF BEDS.

WHERE'S MY MUÑECA— THE ONE I WAS TOLD IS NAMED DORA. THE BIG PEOPLE IN GREEN SAID I SHOULD HOLD HER TIGHT UNTIL I COULD BE WITH MAMÁ AND MI HERMANITO.

THEN I REMEMBER . . . IT WAS SO DARK.
MAMÁ SHOOK ME AND MY LITTLE BROTHER, EMILIO, AWAKE.

¡DESPIÉRTATE!
¡DESPIÉRTATE,
MIJA!

EMILIO WAS SUCKING HIS
THUMB AND HOLDING HIS SCRUFFY
OSITO DE PELUCHE SO TIGHTLY.

MAMI'S EYES DARTED AROUND
THE DARK ROOM. SHE MOVED QUICKLY,
STUFFING SOME TOYS INTO A BAG.

I'D NEVER SEEN HER
WORRIED LIKE THIS.

WHAT ABOUT
LOBITO,
OUR PUPPY?
WHAT ABOUT
MY FIRST DAY
OF PRIMARIA?

IT'S GONNA
BE ALRIGHT,
MI PEQUEÑITA.
WE'RE GONNA
MEET WITH PAPÁ,
EN EL NORTE.

WITH ME AND LITTLE EMILIO ON EITHER SIDE
OF HER, WE HURRIED ACROSS THE STREETS.

NO HABÍA NADIE AFUERA.

TODO ESTABA SILENCIOSO.

WE WALKED PAST OUR TÍA'S TIENDA
OVER ON CALLE JUAN ALDAMA AND
CROSSED TO CALLE IGNACIO ALLENDE
WHERE I WAS SUPPOSED TO
GO TO SCHOOL IN A FEW DAYS.

THEN UNAS POCAS CUADRAS MÁS ADELANTE
I SAW BIG PEOPLE HEADING QUICKLY TO A
STREET CORNER AND BEGIN GATHERING.

I HAD NEVER MET ANY OF THEM BEFORE.

WE STOPPED TO JOIN THEM.

MAMÁ WHISPERED SOMETHING TO A MAN.

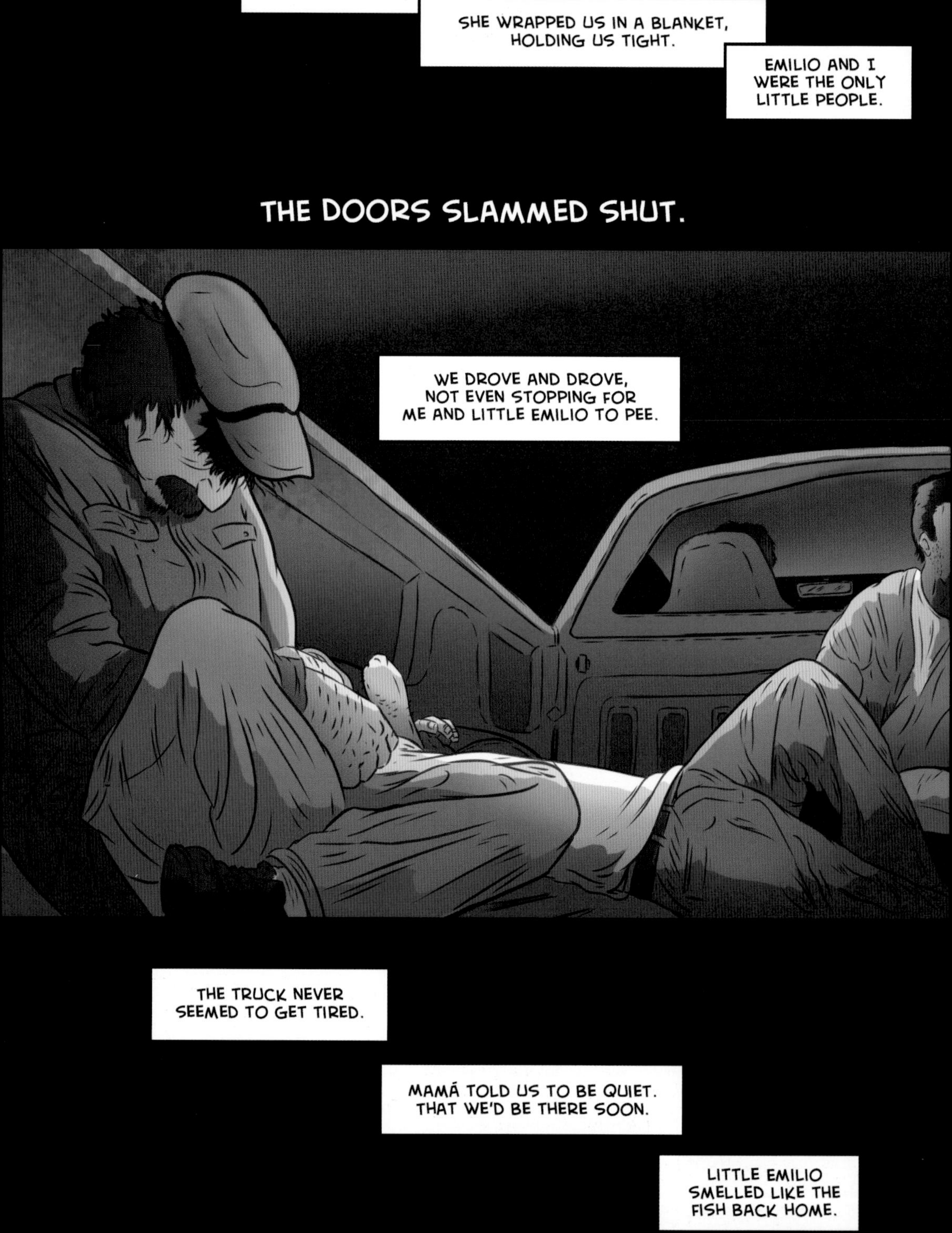
SHE WRAPPED US IN A BLANKET, HOLDING US TIGHT.
EMILIO AND I WERE THE ONLY LITTLE PEOPLE.
THE DOORS SLAMMED SHUT.
WE DROVE AND DROVE, NOT EVEN STOPPING FOR ME AND LITTLE EMILIO TO PEE.
THE TRUCK NEVER SEEMED TO GET TIRED.
MAMÁ TOLD US TO BE QUIET. THAT WE'D BE THERE SOON.
LITTLE EMILIO SMELLED LIKE THE FISH BACK HOME.

THE TRUCK STOPPED.
THE DOORS OPENED.

THE SUN AND WIND
SCRATCHED MY EYES.

DUST CAKED THE
INSIDE OF MY MOUTH.

MAMI CLIMBED DOWN
AND REACHED FOR US,
ONE BY ONE.

WE WAITED.

IT'LL BE OKAY.
WE'RE GOING
TO SEE YOUR
PAPÁ SOON.

THEY TOLD US
TO STAY PUT ALLÍ,
DETRÁS DE LOS
ARBUSTOS Y
LOS ÁRBOLES.

A POCOS PASOS
HABÍA UN RÍO ENORME,
EL MÁS GRANDE
QUE JAMÁS HABÍA VISTO.

AND THEN IT WAS NIGHT AGAIN,
AND MAMI GRABBED US,
ONE IN EACH ARM,
BAG SLUNG OVER HER SHOULDER.

WE FOLLOWED THE BIG PEOPLE
TO THE RIVER'S EDGE.

*"HOLD ONTO THE BALSA. QUICK.
CON MUCHA FUERZA."*

MAMI PUSHED ME AND LITTLE
EMILIO ONTO THE RAFT.

SHE HELD TIGHT TO ITS SIDE,
STRETCHING HER PINKIES FOR OURS.

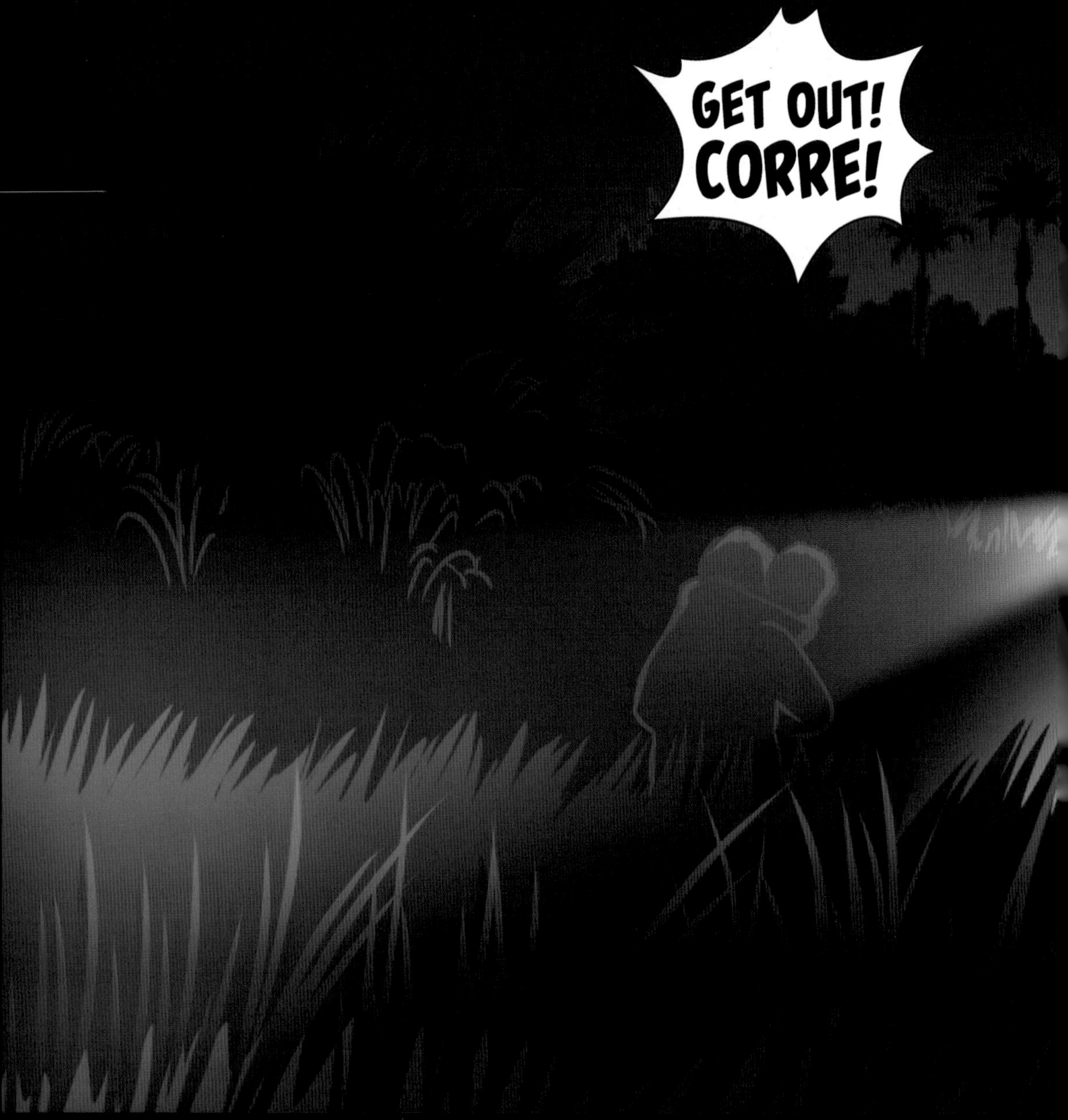
GET OUT! CORRE!

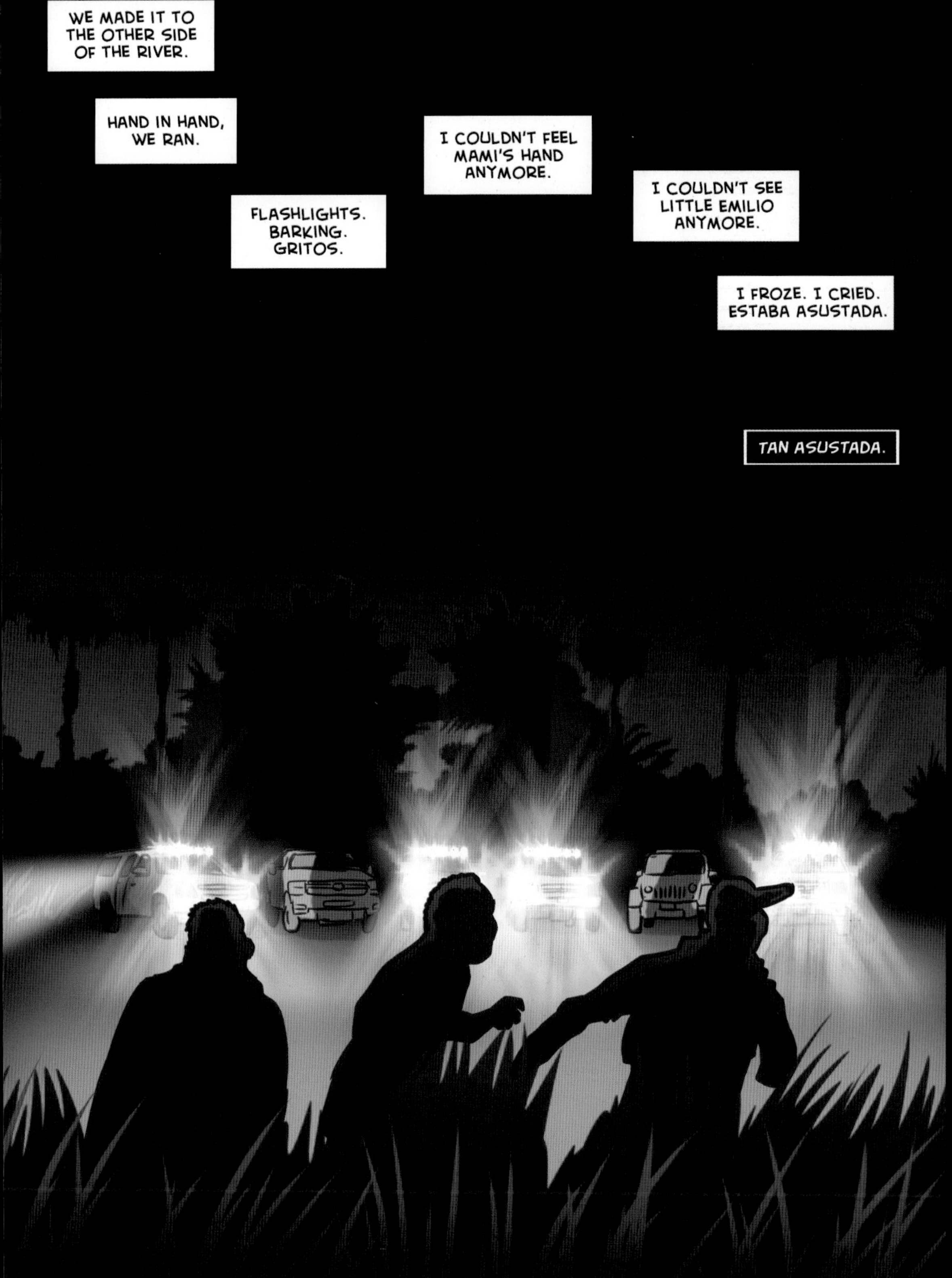
WE MADE IT TO THE OTHER SIDE OF THE RIVER.
HAND IN HAND, WE RAN.
FLASHLIGHTS. BARKING. GRITOS.
I COULDN'T FEEL MAMI'S HAND ANYMORE.
I COULDN'T SEE LITTLE EMILIO ANYMORE.
I FROZE. I CRIED. ESTABA ASUSTADA.
TAN ASUSTADA.

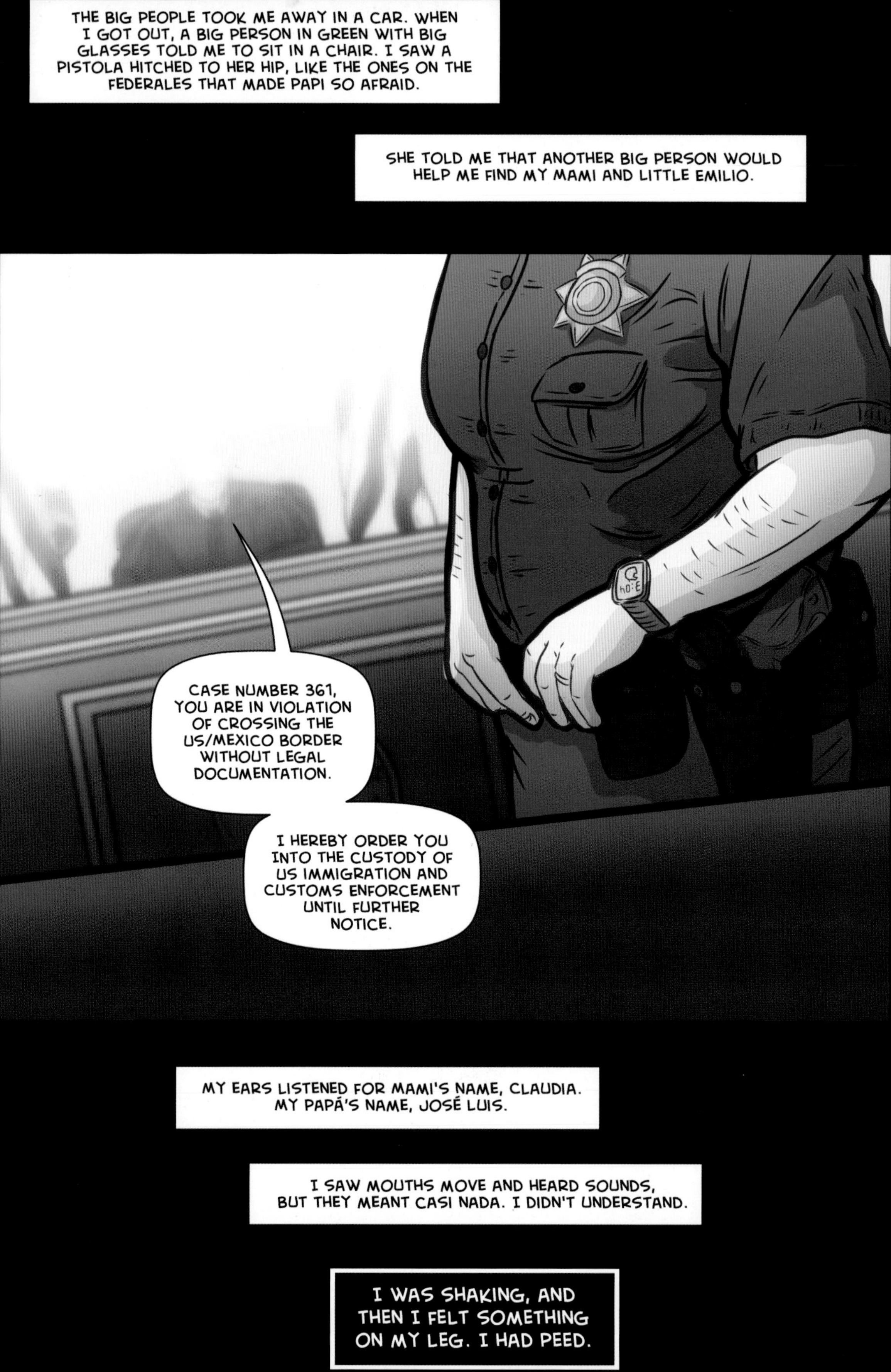
THE BIG PEOPLE TOOK ME AWAY IN A CAR. WHEN I GOT OUT, A BIG PERSON IN GREEN WITH BIG GLASSES TOLD ME TO SIT IN A CHAIR. I SAW A PISTOLA HITCHED TO HER HIP, LIKE THE ONES ON THE FEDERALES THAT MADE PAPI SO AFRAID.
SHE TOLD ME THAT ANOTHER BIG PERSON WOULD HELP ME FIND MY MAMI AND LITTLE EMILIO.
CASE NUMBER 361, YOU ARE IN VIOLATION OF CROSSING THE US/MEXICO BORDER WITHOUT LEGAL DOCUMENTATION.
I HEREBY ORDER YOU INTO THE CUSTODY OF US IMMIGRATION AND CUSTOMS ENFORCEMENT UNTIL FURTHER NOTICE.
MY EARS LISTENED FOR MAMI'S NAME, CLAUDIA. MY PAPÁ'S NAME, JOSÉ LUIS.
I SAW MOUTHS MOVE AND HEARD SOUNDS, BUT THEY MEANT CASI NADA. I DIDN'T UNDERSTAND.
I WAS SHAKING, AND THEN I FELT SOMETHING ON MY LEG. I HAD PEED.

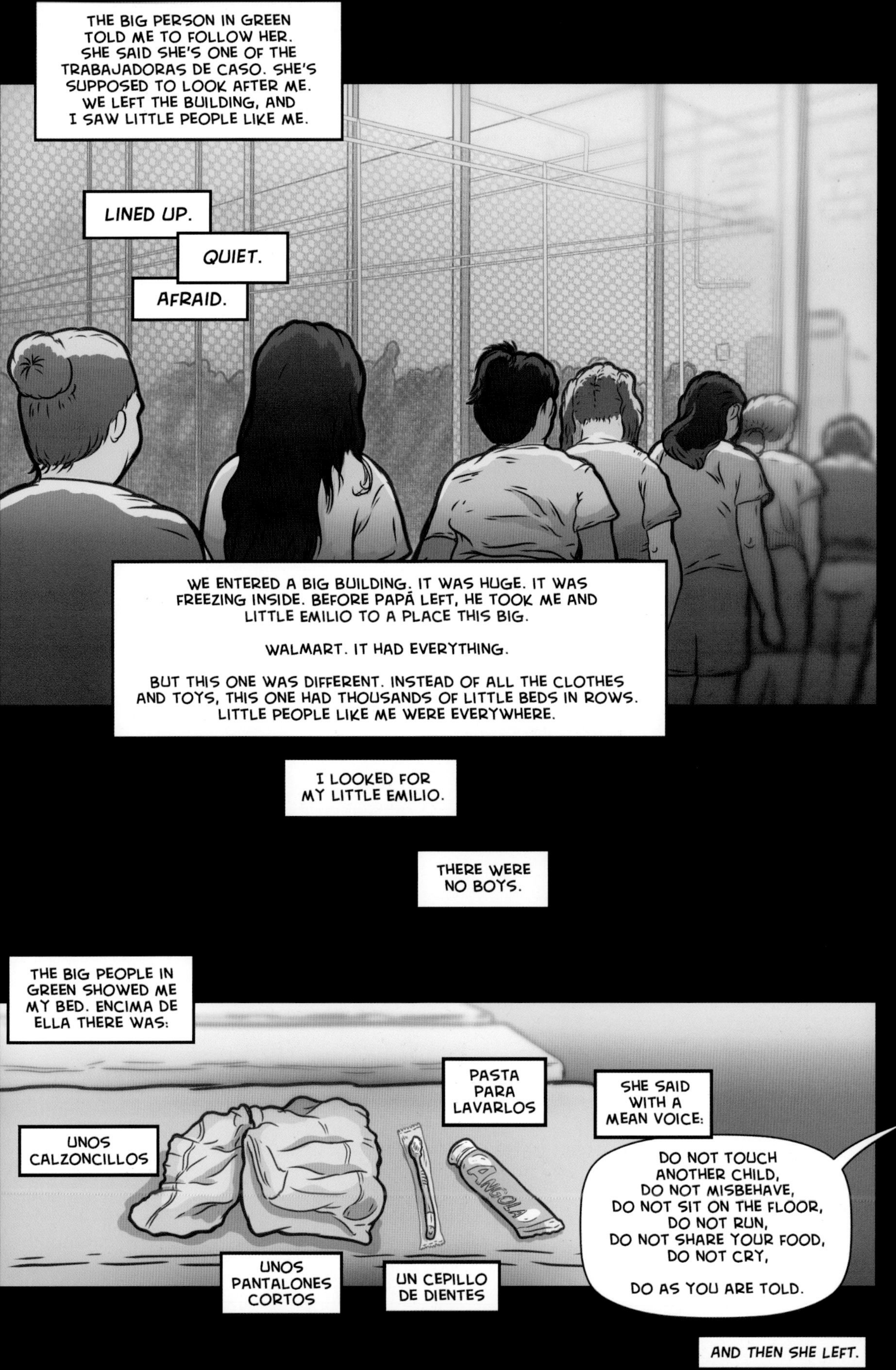

THE BIG PERSON IN GREEN TOLD ME TO FOLLOW HER. SHE SAID SHE'S ONE OF THE TRABAJADORAS DE CASO. SHE'S SUPPOSED TO LOOK AFTER ME. WE LEFT THE BUILDING, AND I SAW LITTLE PEOPLE LIKE ME.
LINED UP.
QUIET.
AFRAID.
WE ENTERED A BIG BUILDING. IT WAS HUGE. IT WAS FREEZING INSIDE. BEFORE PAPÁ LEFT, HE TOOK ME AND LITTLE EMILIO TO A PLACE THIS BIG.
WALMART. IT HAD EVERYTHING.
BUT THIS ONE WAS DIFFERENT. INSTEAD OF ALL THE CLOTHES AND TOYS, THIS ONE HAD THOUSANDS OF LITTLE BEDS IN ROWS. LITTLE PEOPLE LIKE ME WERE EVERYWHERE.
I LOOKED FOR MY LITTLE EMILIO.
THERE WERE NO BOYS.
THE BIG PEOPLE IN GREEN SHOWED ME MY BED. ENCIMA DE ELLA THERE WAS:
UNOS CALZONCILLOS
UNOS PANTALONES CORTOS
UN CEPILLO DE DIENTES
PASTA PARA LAVARLOS
SHE SAID WITH A MEAN VOICE:
DO NOT TOUCH ANOTHER CHILD, DO NOT MISBEHAVE, DO NOT SIT ON THE FLOOR, DO NOT RUN, DO NOT SHARE YOUR FOOD, DO NOT CRY,
DO AS YOU ARE TOLD.
AND THEN SHE LEFT.

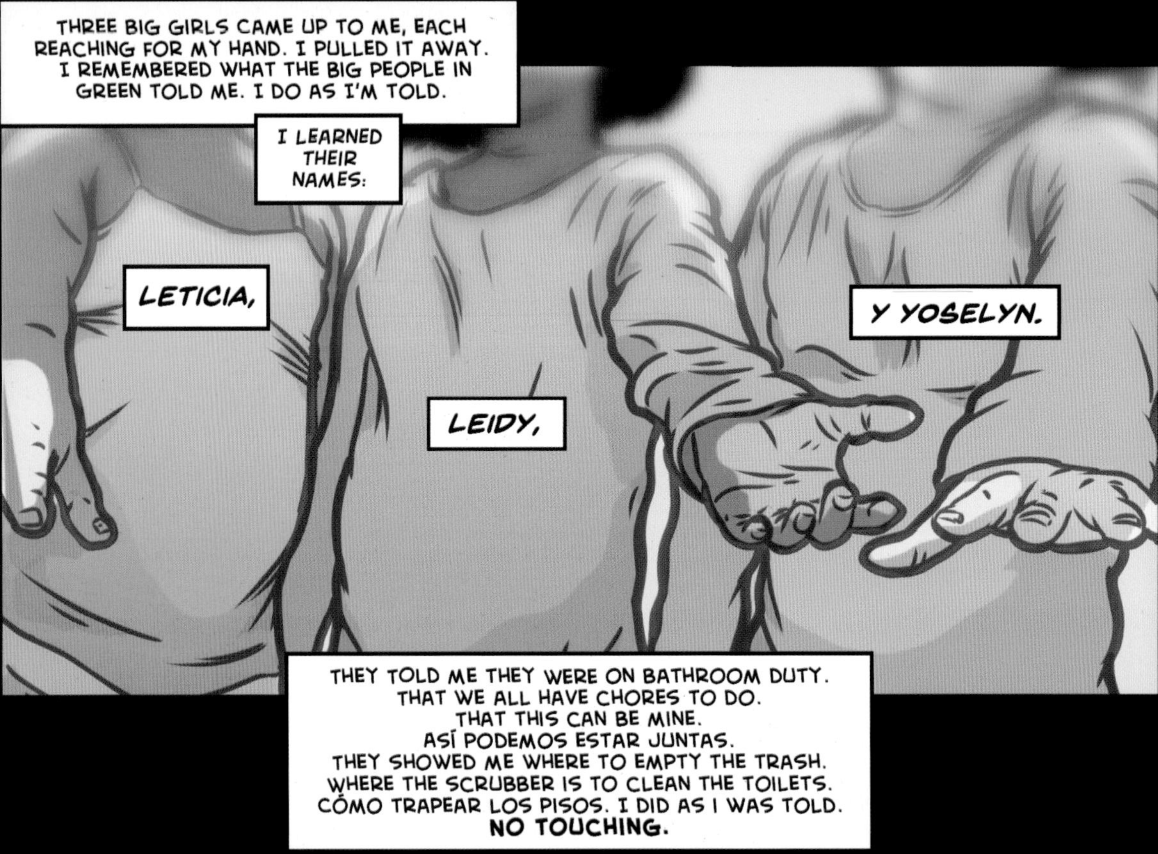
THREE BIG GIRLS CAME UP TO ME, EACH REACHING FOR MY HAND. I PULLED IT AWAY. I REMEMBERED WHAT THE BIG PEOPLE IN GREEN TOLD ME. I DO AS I'M TOLD.
I LEARNED THEIR NAMES:
LETICIA,
LEIDY,
Y YOSELYN.
THEY TOLD ME THEY WERE ON BATHROOM DUTY. THAT WE ALL HAVE CHORES TO DO. THAT THIS CAN BE MINE. ASÍ PODEMOS ESTAR JUNTAS. THEY SHOWED ME WHERE TO EMPTY THE TRASH. WHERE THE SCRUBBER IS TO CLEAN THE TOILETS. CÓMO TRAPEAR LOS PISOS. I DID AS I WAS TOLD. NO TOUCHING.

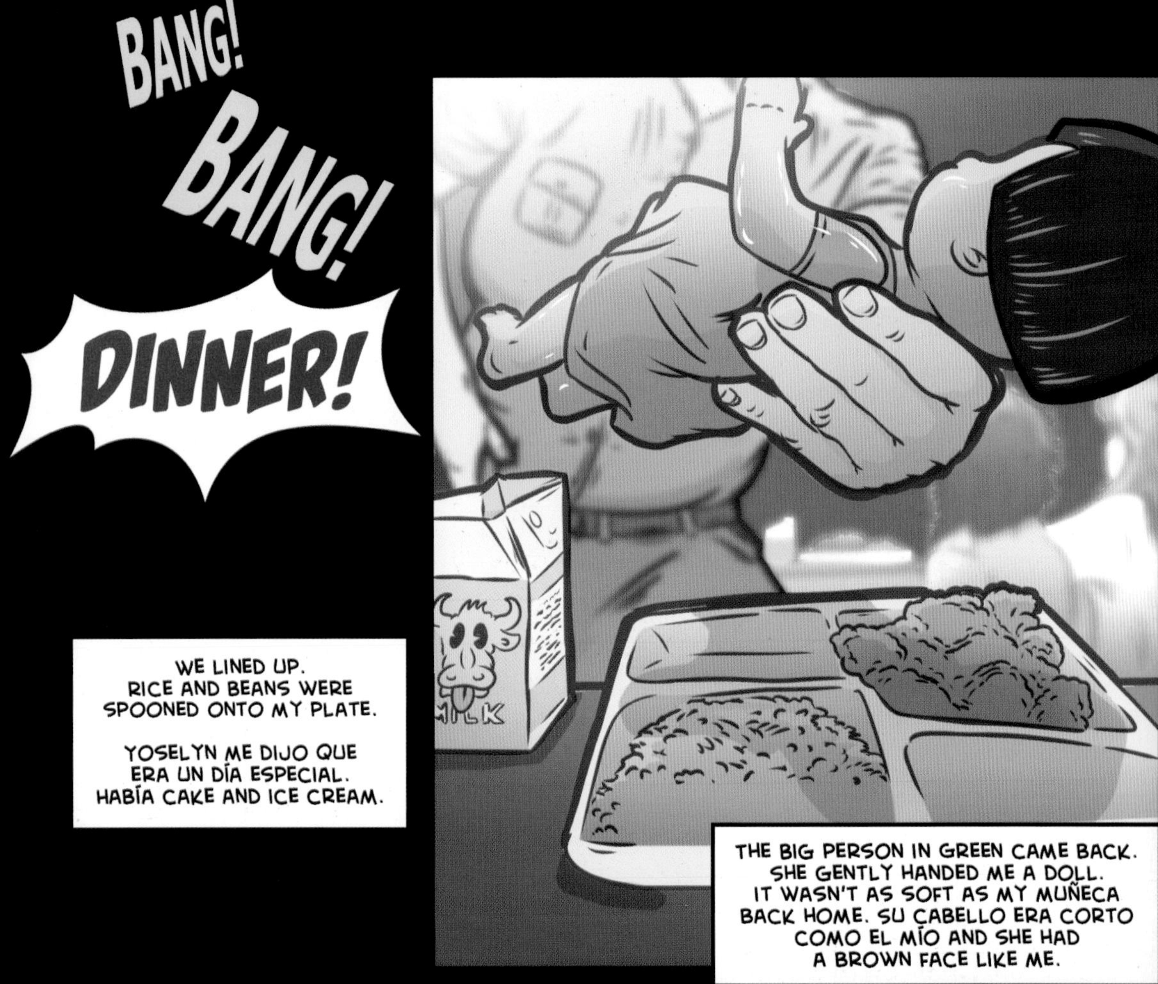
BANG!
BANG!
DINNER!
WE LINED UP. RICE AND BEANS WERE SPOONED ONTO MY PLATE.
YOSELYN ME DIJO QUE ERA UN DÍA ESPECIAL. HABÍA CAKE AND ICE CREAM.
MILK
THE BIG PERSON IN GREEN CAME BACK. SHE GENTLY HANDED ME A DOLL. IT WASN'T AS SOFT AS MY MUÑECA BACK HOME. SU CABELLO ERA CORTO COMO EL MÍO AND SHE HAD A BROWN FACE LIKE ME.

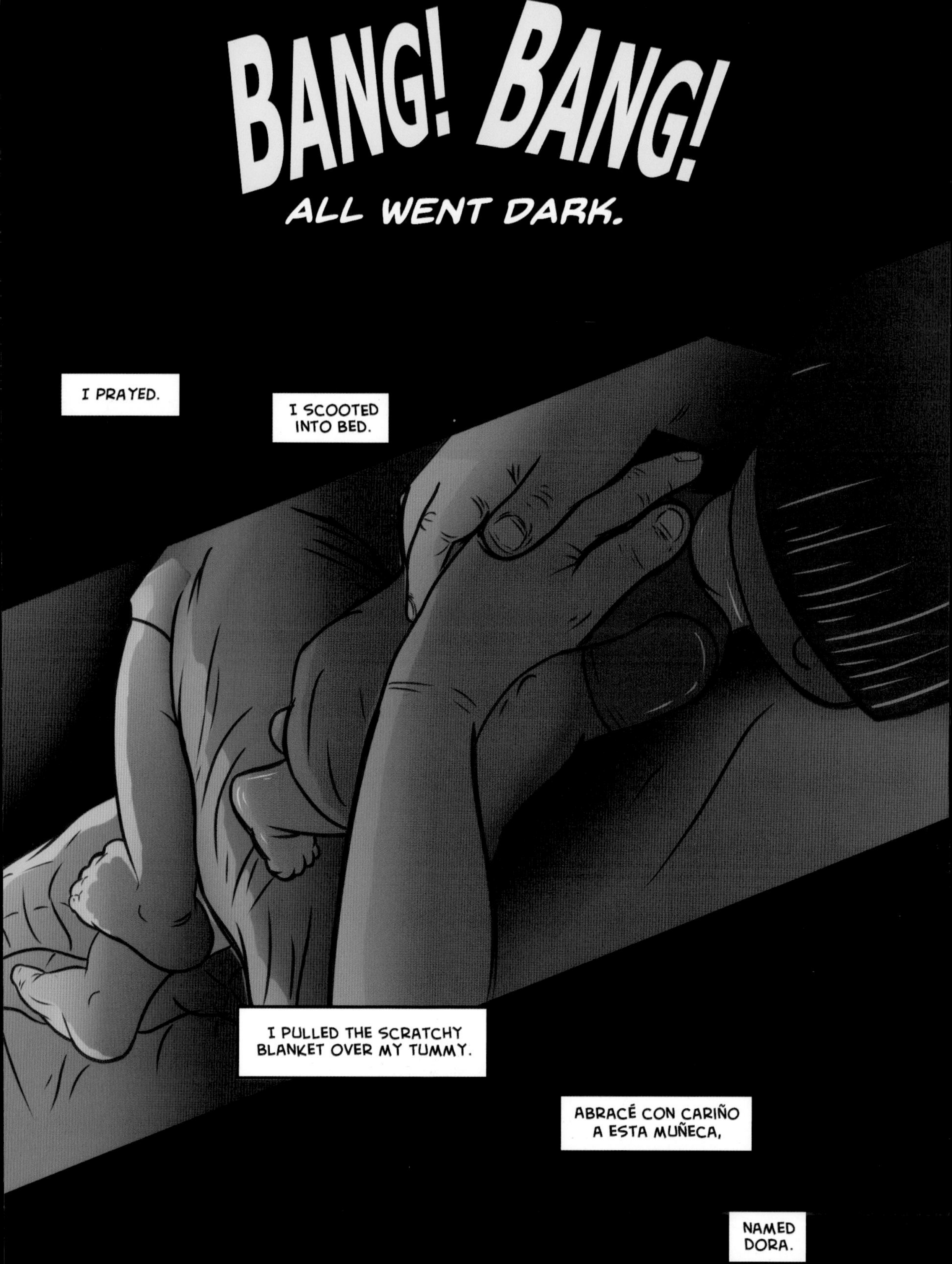
BANG! BANG!
ALL WENT DARK.
I PRAYED.
I SCOOTED INTO BED.
I PULLED THE SCRATCHY BLANKET OVER MY TUMMY.
ABRACÉ CON CARIÑO A ESTA MUÑECA,
NAMED DORA.

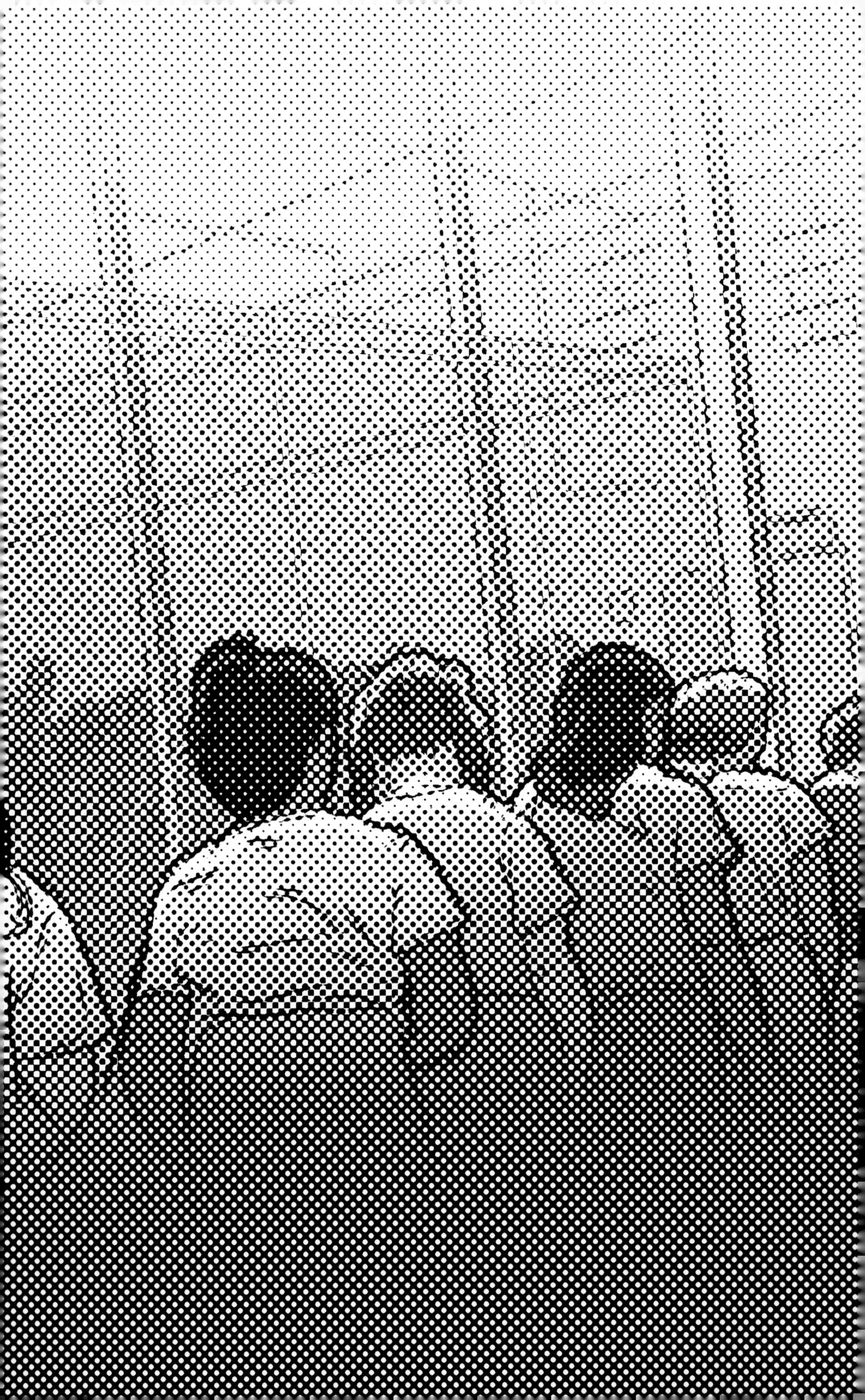

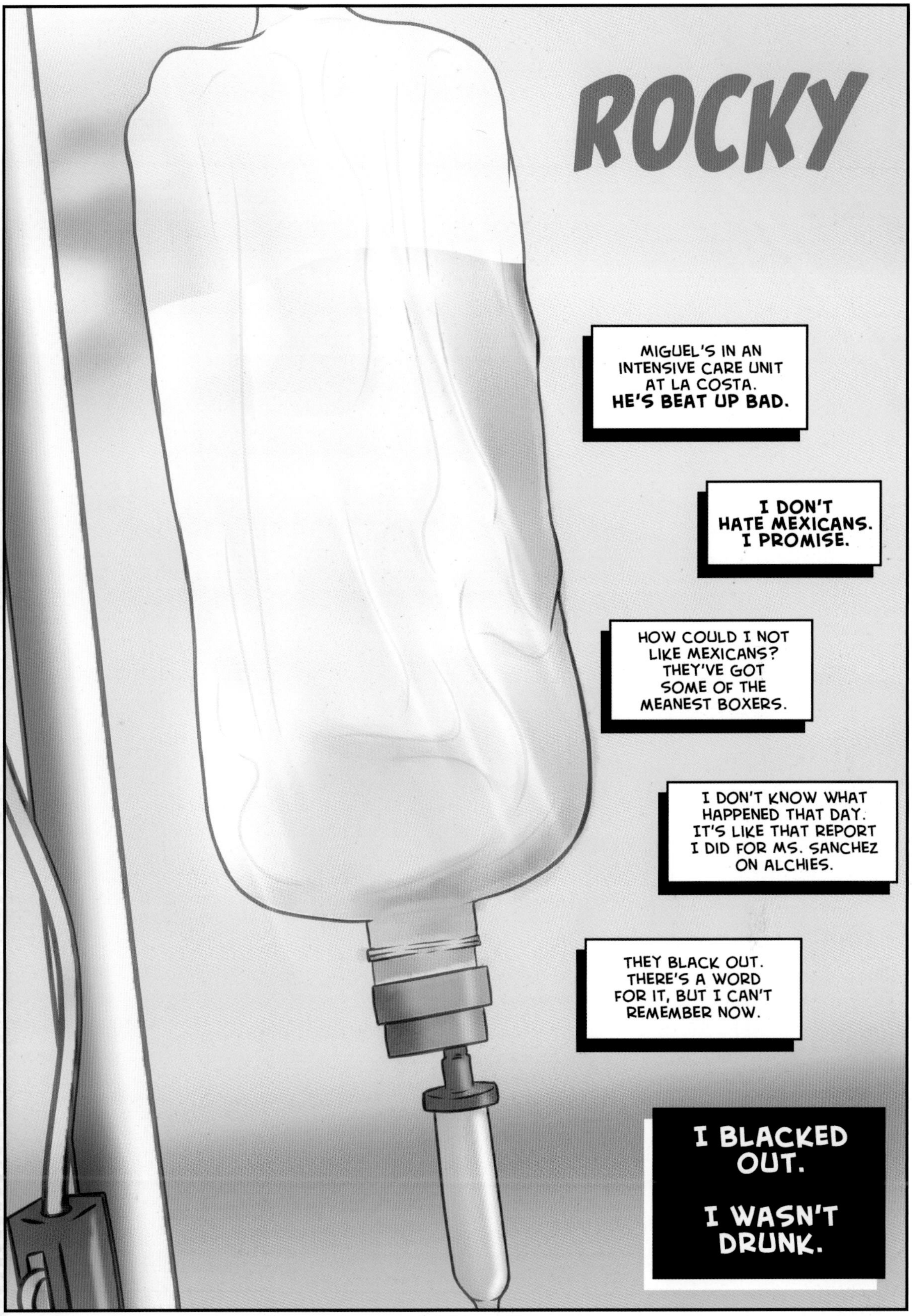
ROCKY
MIGUEL'S IN AN INTENSIVE CARE UNIT AT LA COSTA. HE'S BEAT UP BAD.
I DON'T HATE MEXICANS. I PROMISE.
HOW COULD I NOT LIKE MEXICANS? THEY'VE GOT SOME OF THE MEANEST BOXERS.
I DON'T KNOW WHAT HAPPENED THAT DAY. IT'S LIKE THAT REPORT I DID FOR MS. SANCHEZ ON ALCHIES.
THEY BLACK OUT. THERE'S A WORD FOR IT, BUT I CAN'T REMEMBER NOW.
I BLACKED OUT.
I WASN'T DRUNK.

MY NAME IS RODDEL ROXY. I'M A PASTY-FACED, CHUBBY WHITE KID SURVIVING IN THIS GODFORSAKEN BORDER TOWN THEY CALL CALEXICO.
SCHOOL ZONE ZONA ESCOLAR
CALEXICO HIGH SCHOOL
I DIDN'T ALWAYS LIVE HERE. WE MOVED JUST BEFORE 9TH GRADE.
UNTIL THEN I'D LIVED IN BORREGO SPRINGS.
MY MOM WAS A MANAGER AT THE DESERT INN.
RODDEL THE THIRD, MY DAD, WELL, HE WAS A COP, JUST LIKE HIS DAD AND HIS GRANDAD.
I KNEW I DIDN'T WANT TO BE A COP,
BUT I NEVER THOUGHT I'D FIND MYSELF YANKED AWAY FROM THE FRIENDS I'D HAD SINCE FOREVER.
I THOUGHT IT WAS BORREGO FOR LIFE.
IT HAPPENED THE SUMMER BEFORE 9TH GRADE...
MOM LEFT DAD. IT TURNS OUT, HE'D BEEN MESSING AROUND WITH HER BEST FRIEND, SHELLY. EVERYBODY SEEMED TO KNOW, EXCEPT MOM. UNTIL SHE DID.
YOU CAN PACK UP AND MOVE WITH ME TO SACRAMENTO,
WE'LL STAY WITH YOUR GRANDMA TILL WE GET SETTLED.
SHE GAVE ME A CHOICE:
OR
YOU CAN STAY HERE WITH YOUR JACKASS OF A DAD.
I CHOSE DAD.

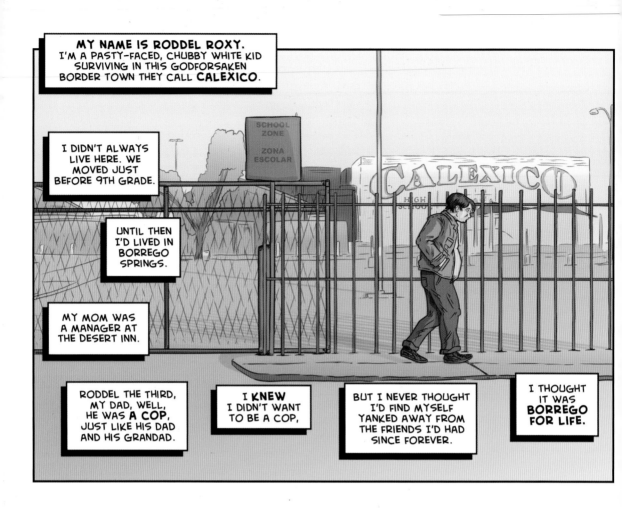

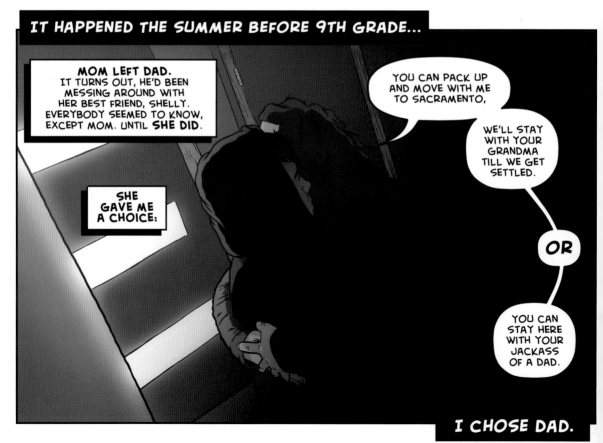

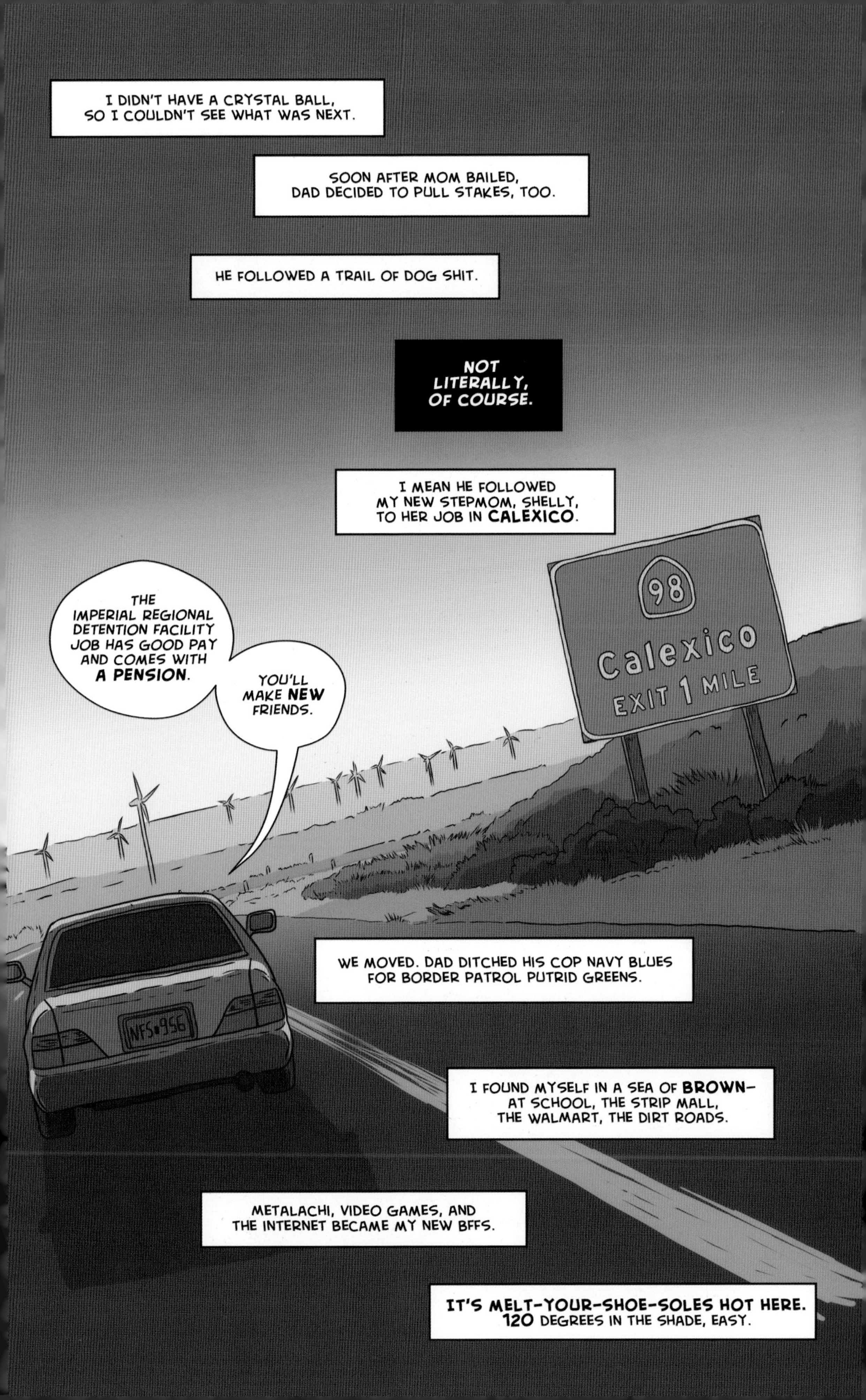
I DIDN'T HAVE A CRYSTAL BALL, SO I COULDN'T SEE WHAT WAS NEXT.
SOON AFTER MOM BAILED, DAD DECIDED TO PULL STAKES, TOO.
HE FOLLOWED A TRAIL OF DOG SHIT.
NOT LITERALLY, OF COURSE.
I MEAN HE FOLLOWED MY NEW STEPMOM, SHELLY, TO HER JOB IN CALEXICO.
98
Calexico
EXIT 1 MILE
THE IMPERIAL REGIONAL DETENTION FACILITY JOB HAS GOOD PAY AND COMES WITH A PENSION.
YOU'LL MAKE NEW FRIENDS.
NFS•956
WE MOVED. DAD DITCHED HIS COP NAVY BLUES FOR BORDER PATROL PUTRID GREENS.
I FOUND MYSELF IN A SEA OF BROWN—AT SCHOOL, THE STRIP MALL, THE WALMART, THE DIRT ROADS.
METALACHI, VIDEO GAMES, AND THE INTERNET BECAME MY NEW BFFS.
IT'S MELT-YOUR-SHOE-SOLES HOT HERE. 120 DEGREES IN THE SHADE, EASY.

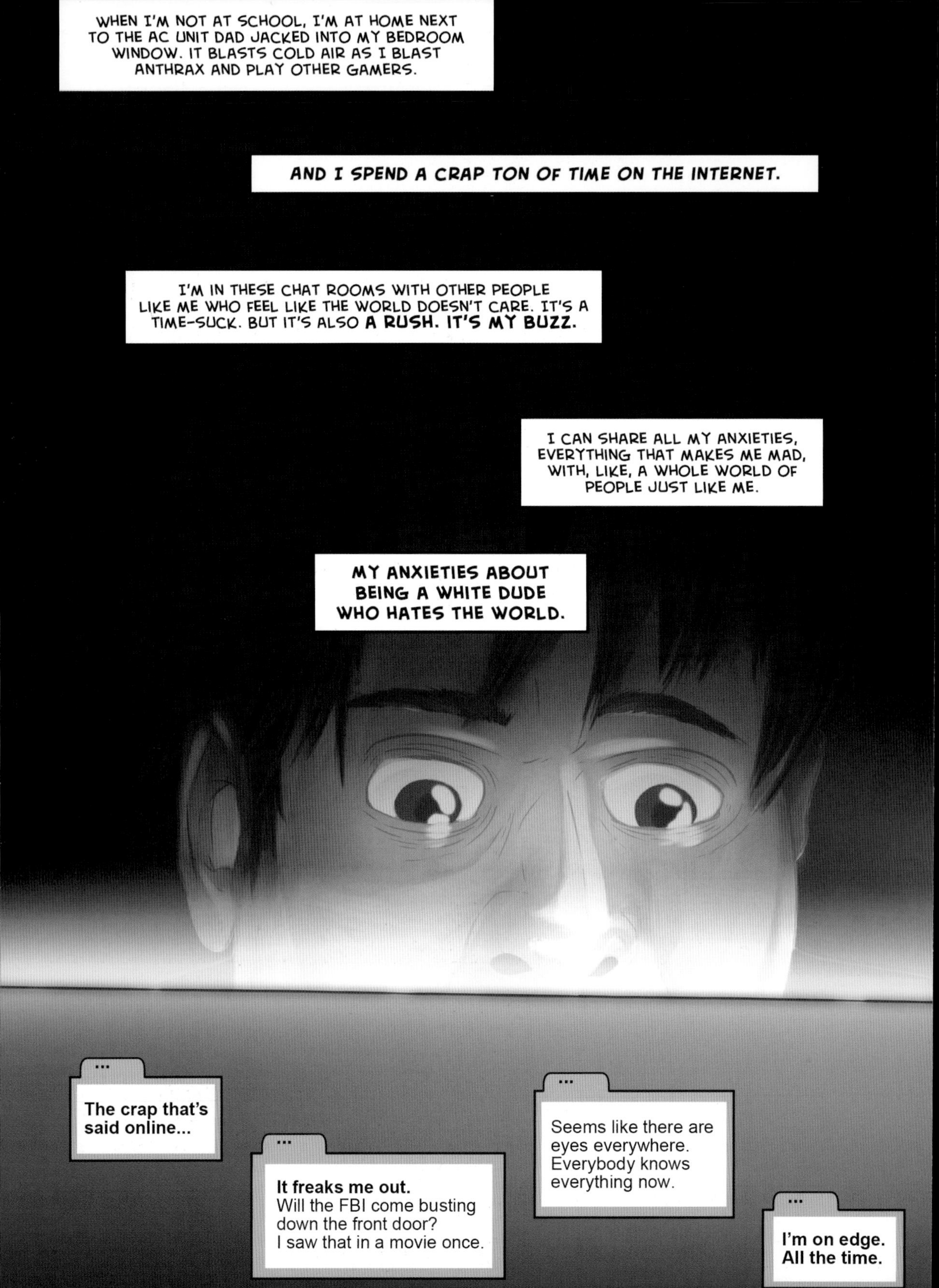
WHEN I'M NOT AT SCHOOL, I'M AT HOME NEXT TO THE AC UNIT DAD JACKED INTO MY BEDROOM WINDOW. IT BLASTS COLD AIR AS I BLAST ANTHRAX AND PLAY OTHER GAMERS.
AND I SPEND A CRAP TON OF TIME ON THE INTERNET.
I'M IN THESE CHAT ROOMS WITH OTHER PEOPLE LIKE ME WHO FEEL LIKE THE WORLD DOESN'T CARE. IT'S A TIME-SUCK. BUT IT'S ALSO A RUSH. IT'S MY BUZZ.
I CAN SHARE ALL MY ANXIETIES, EVERYTHING THAT MAKES ME MAD, WITH, LIKE, A WHOLE WORLD OF PEOPLE JUST LIKE ME.
MY ANXIETIES ABOUT BEING A WHITE DUDE WHO HATES THE WORLD.
...
The crap that's said online...
...
It freaks me out. Will the FBI come busting down the front door? I saw that in a movie once.
...
Seems like there are eyes everywhere. Everybody knows everything now.
...
I'm on edge. All the time.

THERE IS THIS ONE GIRL AT SCHOOL, **MARISSA**. SHE CHEERS FOR OUR FOOTBALL TEAM, *THE CALEXICO HIGH BULLDOGS.*

I SEE HER BROTHER, **MIGUEL**, WITH HANDFULS OF BOOKS.

I THINK ABOUT HER AT NIGHT.

THINKING ABOUT HER CALMS ME DOWN WHEN I'M FEELING ESPECIALLY FREAKED OUT.

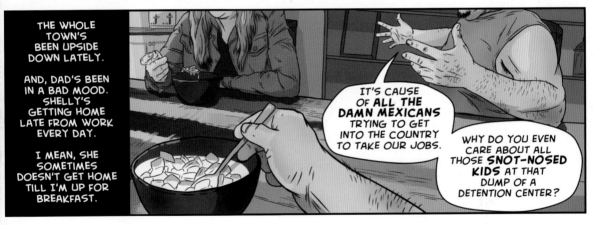

THE WHOLE TOWN'S BEEN UPSIDE DOWN LATELY.

AND, DAD'S BEEN IN A BAD MOOD. SHELLY'S GETTING HOME LATE FROM WORK EVERY DAY.

I MEAN, SHE SOMETIMES DOESN'T GET HOME TILL I'M UP FOR BREAKFAST.

IT'S CAUSE OF **ALL THE DAMN MEXICANS** TRYING TO GET INTO THE COUNTRY TO TAKE OUR JOBS.

WHY DO YOU EVEN CARE ABOUT ALL THOSE **SNOT-NOSED KIDS** AT THAT DUMP OF A DETENTION CENTER?

DAD'S MOSTLY UPSET CAUSE HE HAS TO GRAB HIS OWN BEER FROM THE FRIDGE.

HE HAS TO COOK, TOO.

AT LEAST WHAT HE **THINKS** IS COOKING. HEATING UP A FROZEN PIZZA IN THE MICROWAVE.

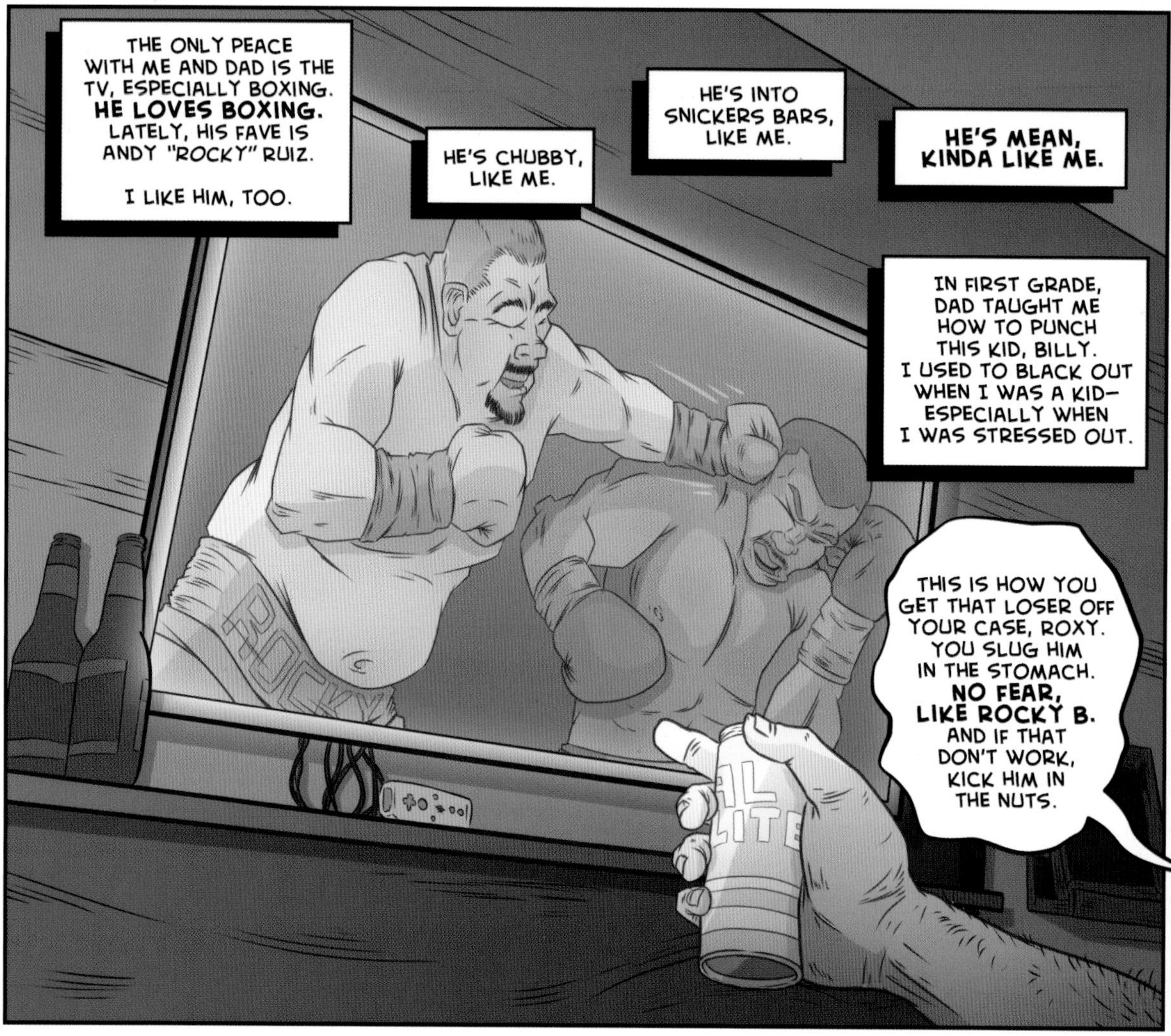
THE ONLY PEACE WITH ME AND DAD IS THE TV, ESPECIALLY BOXING. **HE LOVES BOXING.** LATELY, HIS FAVE IS ANDY "ROCKY" RUIZ.
I LIKE HIM, TOO.
HE'S CHUBBY, LIKE ME.
HE'S INTO SNICKERS BARS, LIKE ME.
HE'S MEAN, KINDA LIKE ME.
IN FIRST GRADE, DAD TAUGHT ME HOW TO PUNCH THIS KID, BILLY. I USED TO BLACK OUT WHEN I WAS A KID— ESPECIALLY WHEN I WAS STRESSED OUT.
THIS IS HOW YOU GET THAT LOSER OFF YOUR CASE, ROXY. YOU SLUG HIM IN THE STOMACH. **NO FEAR, LIKE ROCKY B.** AND IF THAT DON'T WORK, KICK HIM IN THE NUTS.
ROCKY

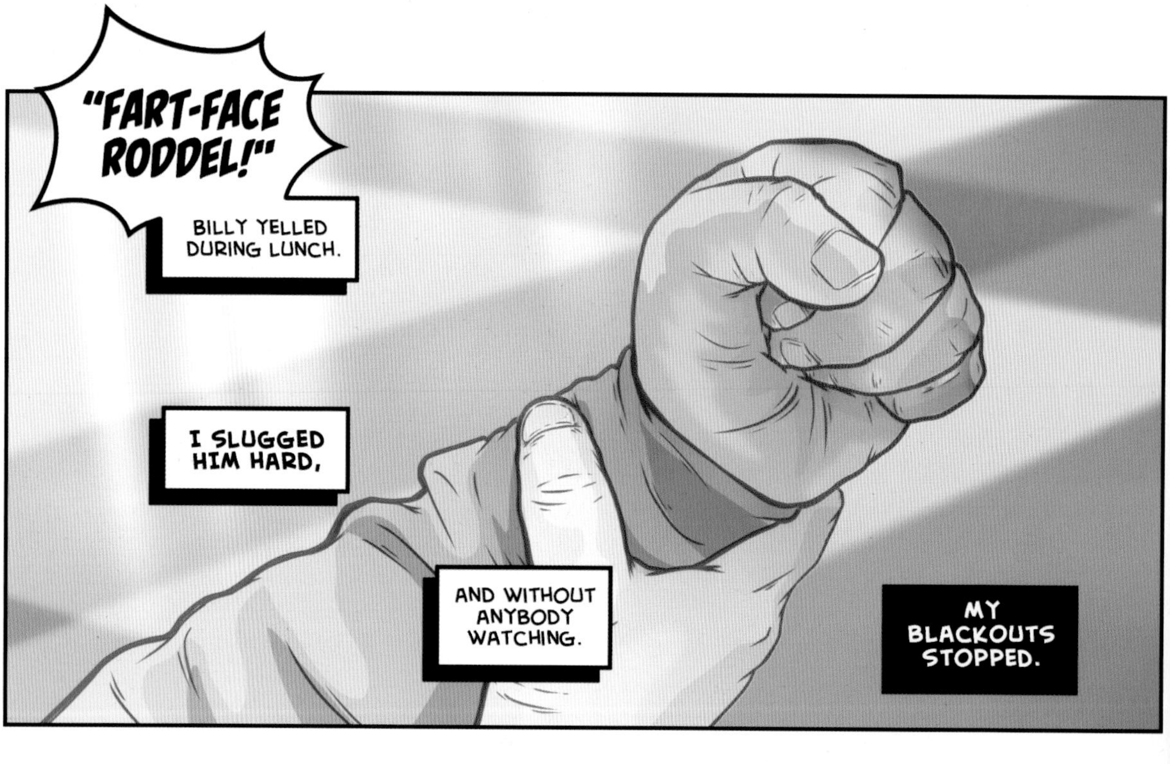
"FART-FACE RODDEL!"
BILLY YELLED DURING LUNCH.
I SLUGGED HIM HARD,
AND WITHOUT ANYBODY WATCHING.
MY BLACKOUTS STOPPED.

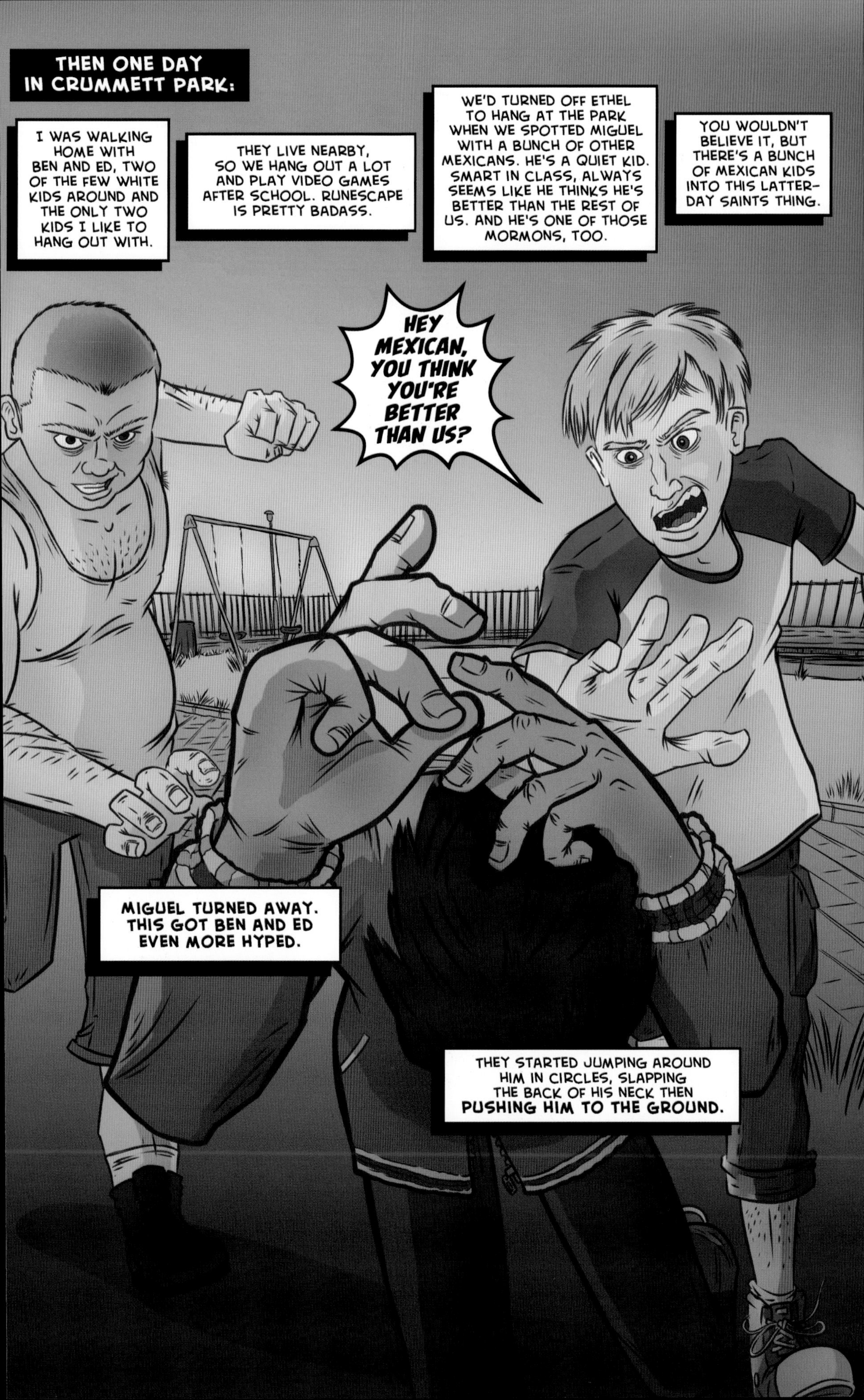
THEN ONE DAY IN CRUMMETT PARK:
I WAS WALKING HOME WITH BEN AND ED, TWO OF THE FEW WHITE KIDS AROUND AND THE ONLY TWO KIDS I LIKE TO HANG OUT WITH.
THEY LIVE NEARBY, SO WE HANG OUT A LOT AND PLAY VIDEO GAMES AFTER SCHOOL. RUNESCAPE IS PRETTY BADASS.
WE'D TURNED OFF ETHEL TO HANG AT THE PARK WHEN WE SPOTTED MIGUEL WITH A BUNCH OF OTHER MEXICANS. HE'S A QUIET KID. SMART IN CLASS, ALWAYS SEEMS LIKE HE THINKS HE'S BETTER THAN THE REST OF US. AND HE'S ONE OF THOSE MORMONS, TOO.
YOU WOULDN'T BELIEVE IT, BUT THERE'S A BUNCH OF MEXICAN KIDS INTO THIS LATTER-DAY SAINTS THING.
HEY MEXICAN, YOU THINK YOU'RE BETTER THAN US?
MIGUEL TURNED AWAY. THIS GOT BEN AND ED EVEN MORE HYPED.
THEY STARTED JUMPING AROUND HIM IN CIRCLES, SLAPPING THE BACK OF HIS NECK THEN PUSHING HIM TO THE GROUND.

THERE WAS YELPING,

AND CRYING.

THEN SILENCE.

NOTHING.

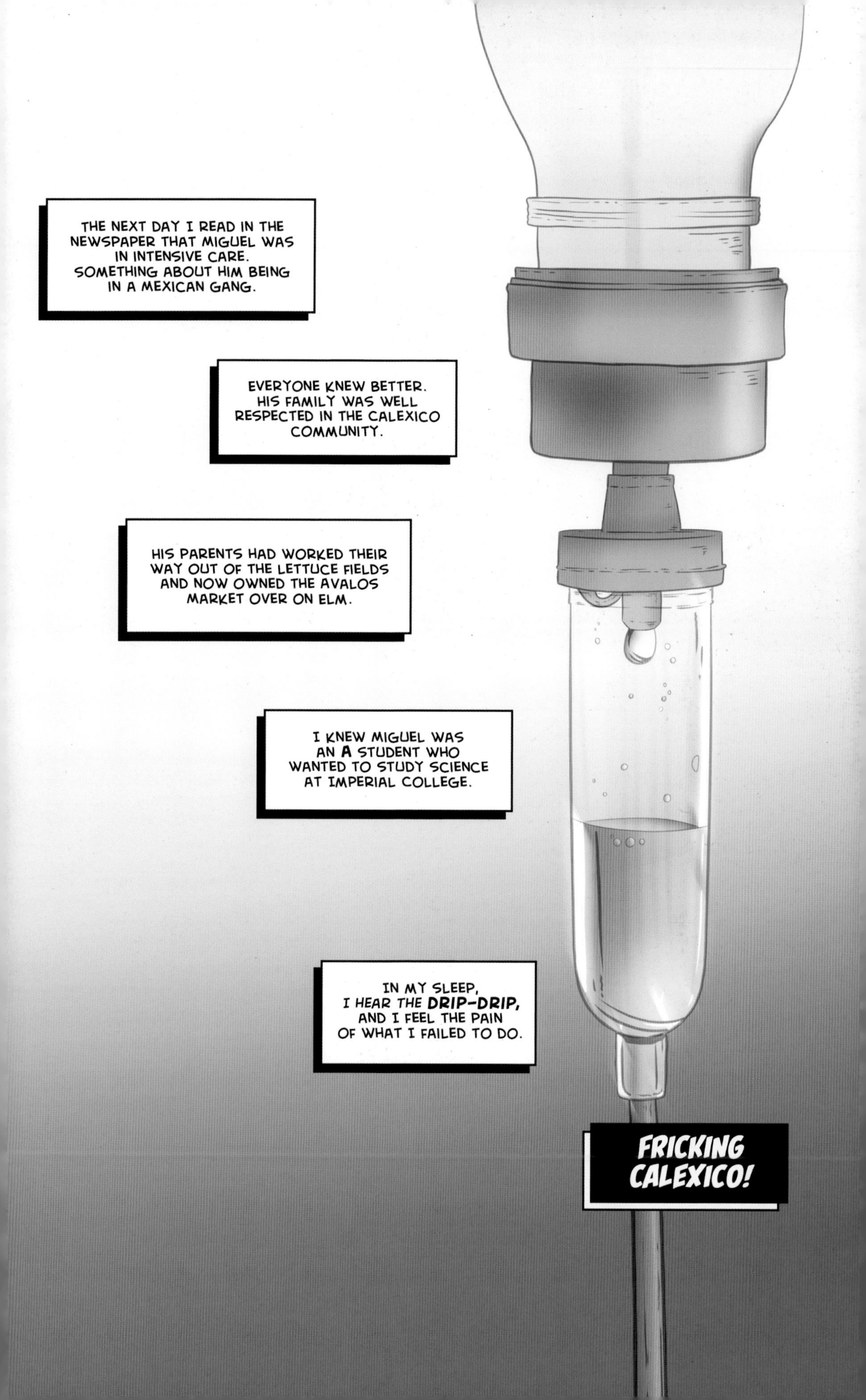
THE NEXT DAY I READ IN THE NEWSPAPER THAT MIGUEL WAS IN INTENSIVE CARE. SOMETHING ABOUT HIM BEING IN A MEXICAN GANG.
EVERYONE KNEW BETTER. HIS FAMILY WAS WELL RESPECTED IN THE CALEXICO COMMUNITY.
HIS PARENTS HAD WORKED THEIR WAY OUT OF THE LETTUCE FIELDS AND NOW OWNED THE AVALOS MARKET OVER ON ELM.
I KNEW MIGUEL WAS AN **A** STUDENT WHO WANTED TO STUDY SCIENCE AT IMPERIAL COLLEGE.
IN MY SLEEP, I HEAR THE **DRIP-DRIP,** AND I FEEL THE PAIN OF WHAT I FAILED TO DO.
FRICKING CALEXICO!

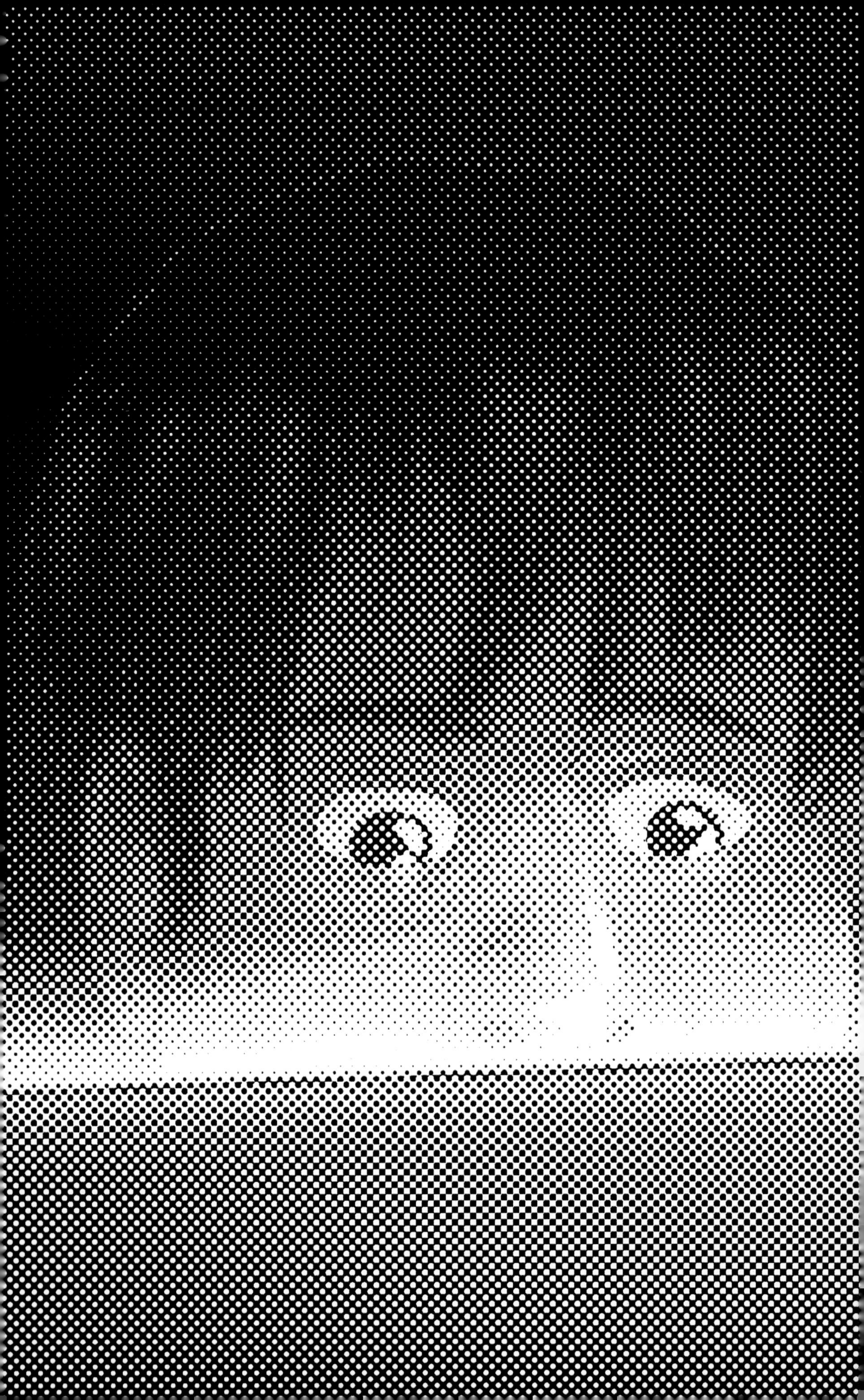

ALBERTO

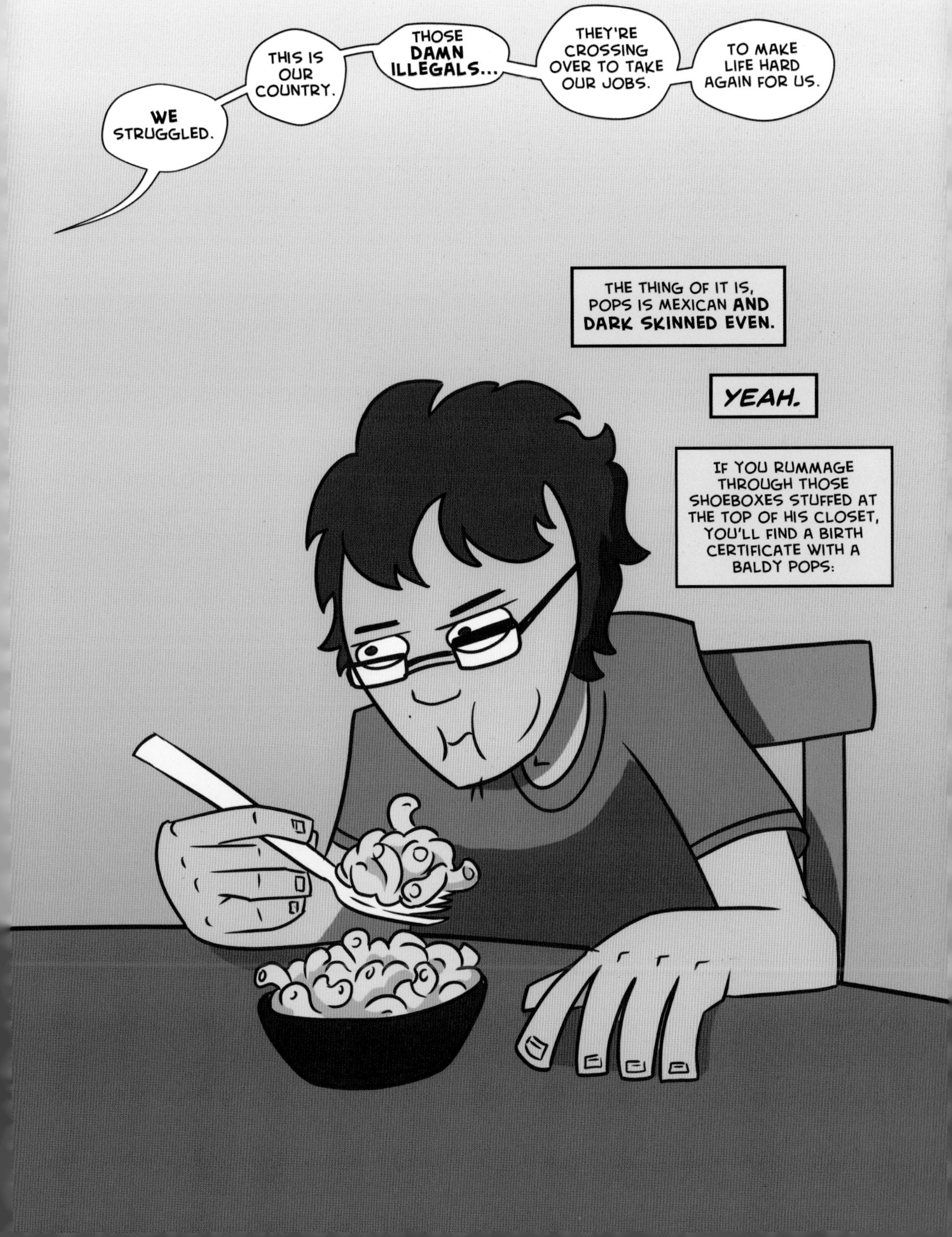

WE STRUGGLED.
THIS IS OUR COUNTRY.
THOSE DAMN ILLEGALS...
THEY'RE CROSSING OVER TO TAKE OUR JOBS.
TO MAKE LIFE HARD AGAIN FOR US.
THE THING OF IT IS, POPS IS MEXICAN AND DARK SKINNED EVEN.
YEAH.
IF YOU RUMMAGE THROUGH THOSE SHOEBOXES STUFFED AT THE TOP OF HIS CLOSET, YOU'LL FIND A BIRTH CERTIFICATE WITH A BALDY POPS:

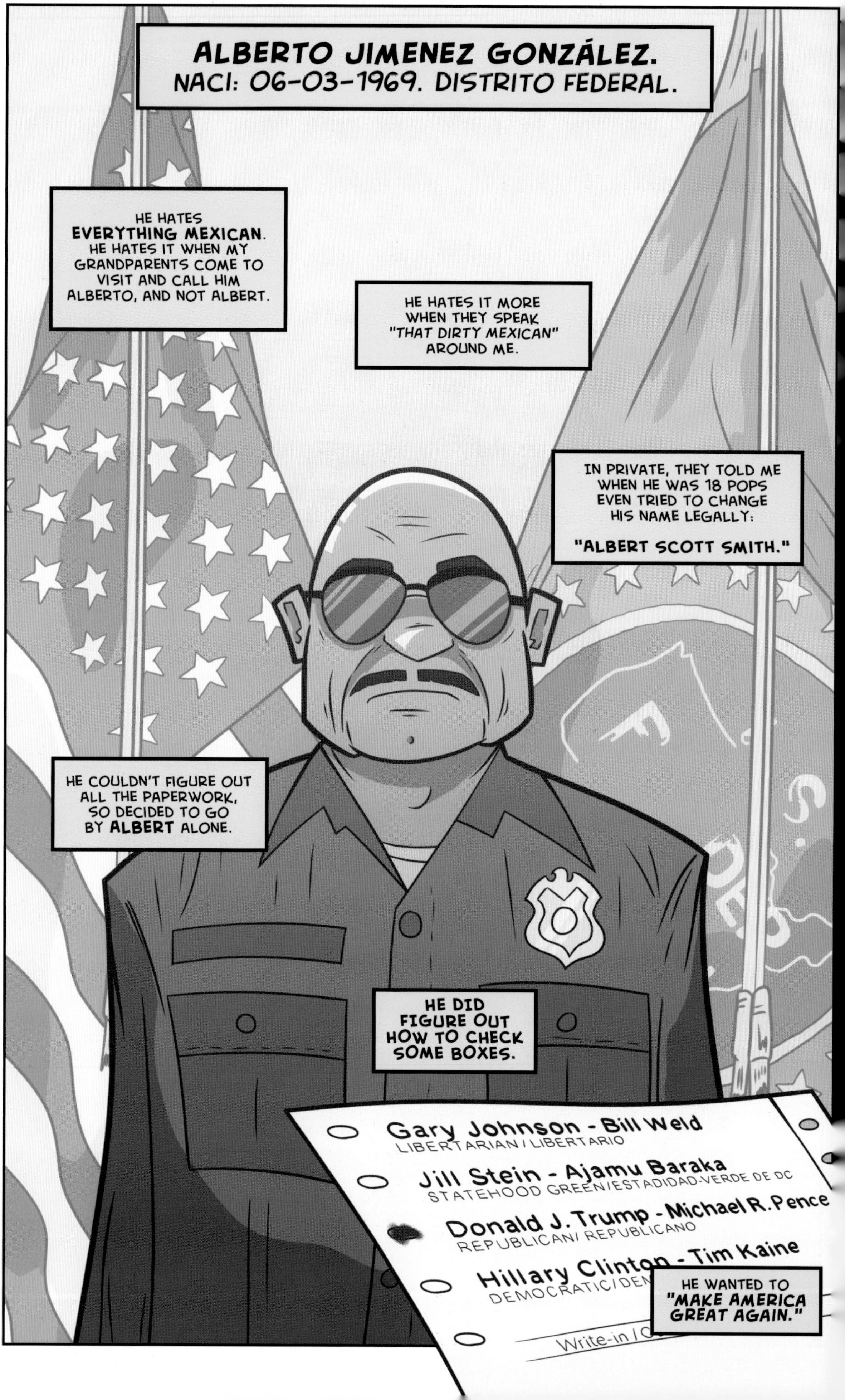
ALBERTO JIMENEZ GONZÁLEZ.
NACI: 06-03-1969. DISTRITO FEDERAL.
HE HATES **EVERYTHING MEXICAN**. HE HATES IT WHEN MY GRANDPARENTS COME TO VISIT AND CALL HIM ALBERTO, AND NOT ALBERT.
HE HATES IT MORE WHEN THEY SPEAK *"THAT DIRTY MEXICAN"* AROUND ME.
IN PRIVATE, THEY TOLD ME WHEN HE WAS 18 POPS EVEN TRIED TO CHANGE HIS NAME LEGALLY:
"ALBERT SCOTT SMITH."
HE COULDN'T FIGURE OUT ALL THE PAPERWORK, SO DECIDED TO GO BY **ALBERT** ALONE.
HE DID FIGURE OUT HOW TO CHECK SOME BOXES.
Gary Johnson - Bill Weld
LIBERTARIAN / LIBERTARIO
Jill Stein - Ajamu Baraka
STATEHOOD GREEN/ESTADIDAD-VERDE DE DC
Donald J. Trump - Michael R. Pence
REPUBLICAN/ REPUBLICANO
Hillary Clinton - Tim Kaine
DEMOCRATIC/DEM
Write-in / O
HE WANTED TO *"MAKE AMERICA GREAT AGAIN."*

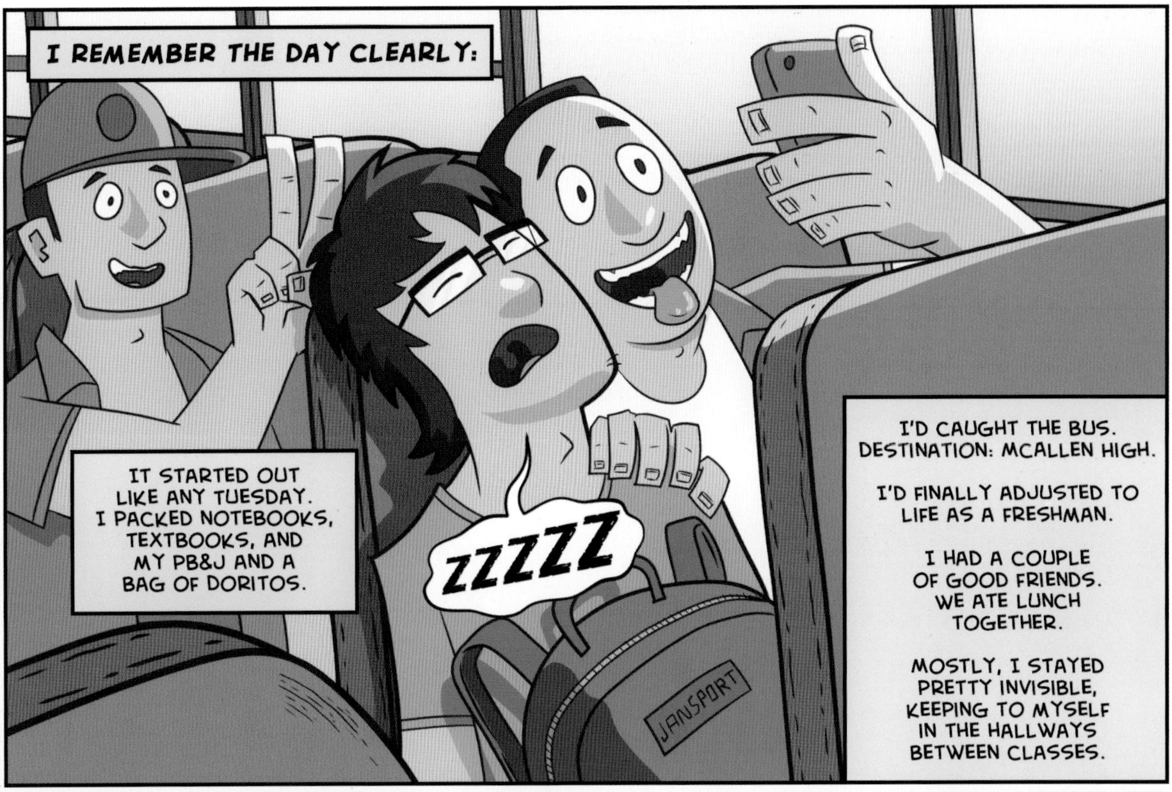
I REMEMBER THE DAY CLEARLY:
IT STARTED OUT LIKE ANY TUESDAY. I PACKED NOTEBOOKS, TEXTBOOKS, AND MY PB&J AND A BAG OF DORITOS.
ZZZZZ
JANSPORT
I'D CAUGHT THE BUS. DESTINATION: MCALLEN HIGH.
I'D FINALLY ADJUSTED TO LIFE AS A FRESHMAN.
I HAD A COUPLE OF GOOD FRIENDS. WE ATE LUNCH TOGETHER.
MOSTLY, I STAYED PRETTY INVISIBLE, KEEPING TO MYSELF IN THE HALLWAYS BETWEEN CLASSES.

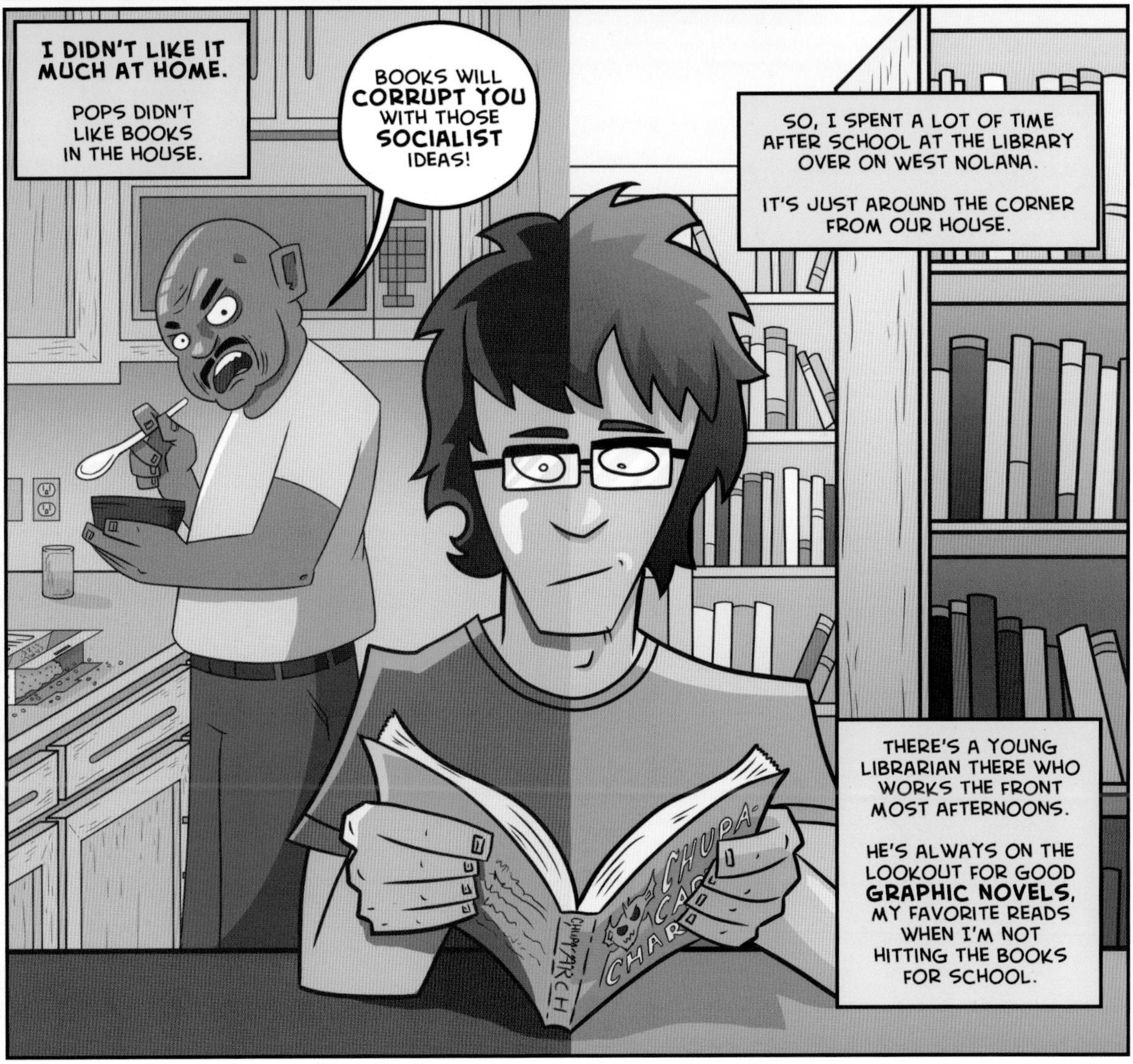
I DIDN'T LIKE IT MUCH AT HOME.
POPS DIDN'T LIKE BOOKS IN THE HOUSE.
BOOKS WILL CORRUPT YOU WITH THOSE SOCIALIST IDEAS!
SO, I SPENT A LOT OF TIME AFTER SCHOOL AT THE LIBRARY OVER ON WEST NOLANA.
IT'S JUST AROUND THE CORNER FROM OUR HOUSE.
THERE'S A YOUNG LIBRARIAN THERE WHO WORKS THE FRONT MOST AFTERNOONS.
HE'S ALWAYS ON THE LOOKOUT FOR GOOD GRAPHIC NOVELS, MY FAVORITE READS WHEN I'M NOT HITTING THE BOOKS FOR SCHOOL.

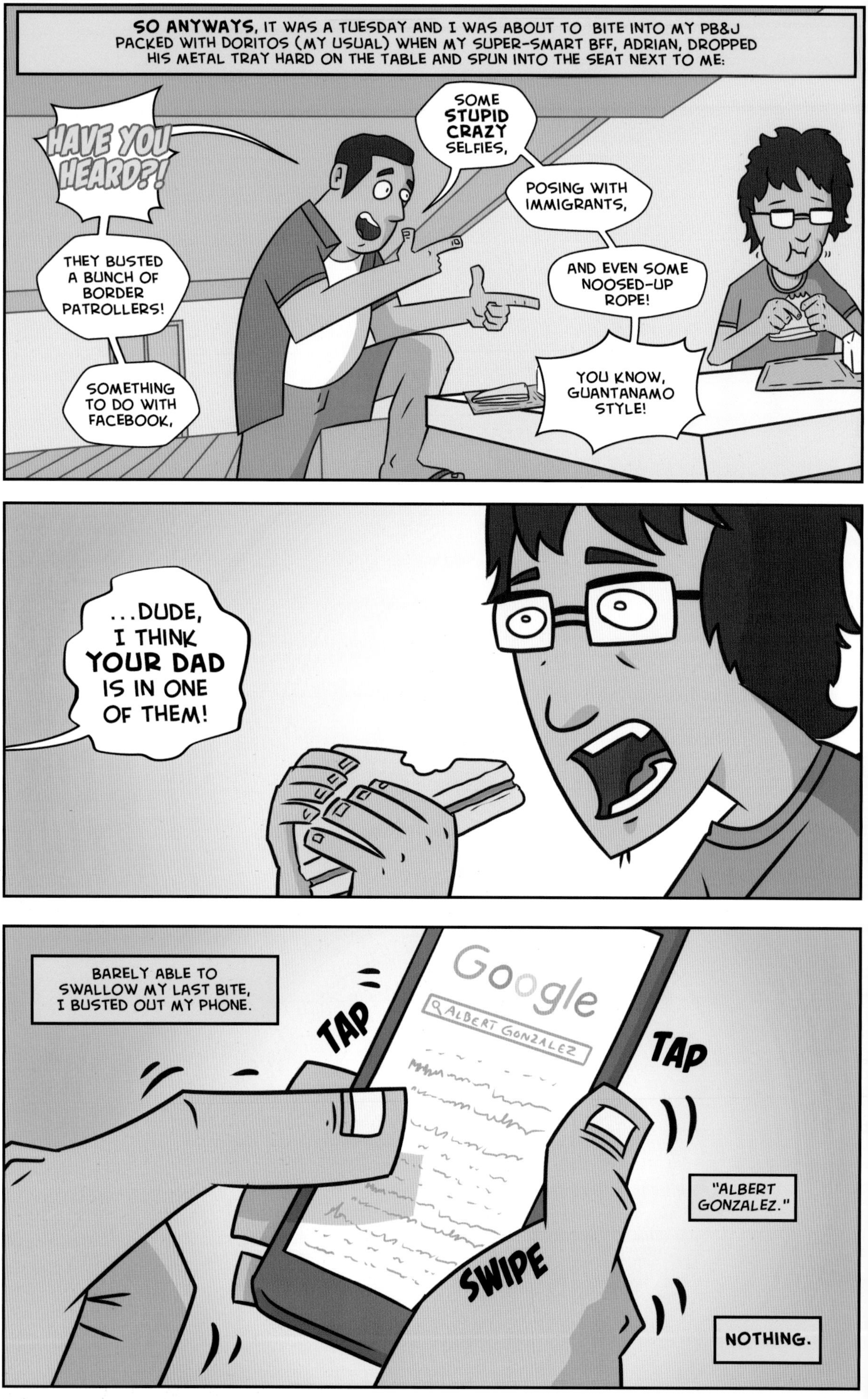
SO ANYWAYS, IT WAS A TUESDAY AND I WAS ABOUT TO BITE INTO MY PB&J PACKED WITH DORITOS (MY USUAL) WHEN MY SUPER-SMART BFF, ADRIAN, DROPPED HIS METAL TRAY HARD ON THE TABLE AND SPUN INTO THE SEAT NEXT TO ME:
HAVE YOU HEARD?!
THEY BUSTED A BUNCH OF BORDER PATROLLERS!
SOMETHING TO DO WITH FACEBOOK,
SOME STUPID CRAZY SELFIES,
POSING WITH IMMIGRANTS,
AND EVEN SOME NOOSED-UP ROPE!
YOU KNOW, GUANTANAMO STYLE!
...DUDE, I THINK YOUR DAD IS IN ONE OF THEM!
BARELY ABLE TO SWALLOW MY LAST BITE, I BUSTED OUT MY PHONE.
TAP
Google
ALBERT GONZALEZ
TAP
"ALBERT GONZALEZ."
SWIPE
NOTHING.

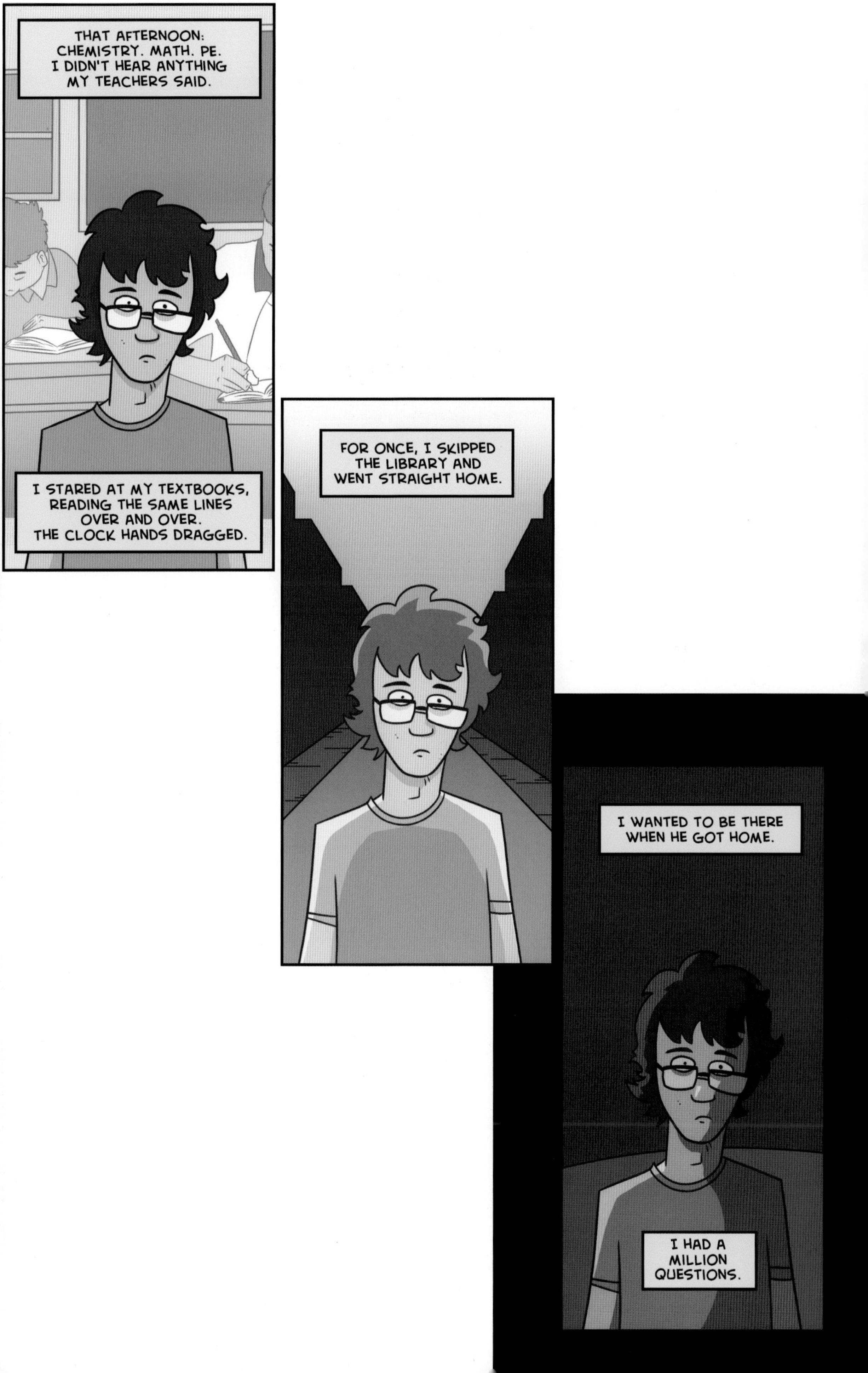
THAT AFTERNOON: CHEMISTRY. MATH. PE. I DIDN'T HEAR ANYTHING MY TEACHERS SAID.
I STARED AT MY TEXTBOOKS, READING THE SAME LINES OVER AND OVER. THE CLOCK HANDS DRAGGED.
FOR ONCE, I SKIPPED THE LIBRARY AND WENT STRAIGHT HOME.
I WANTED TO BE THERE WHEN HE GOT HOME.
I HAD A MILLION QUESTIONS.

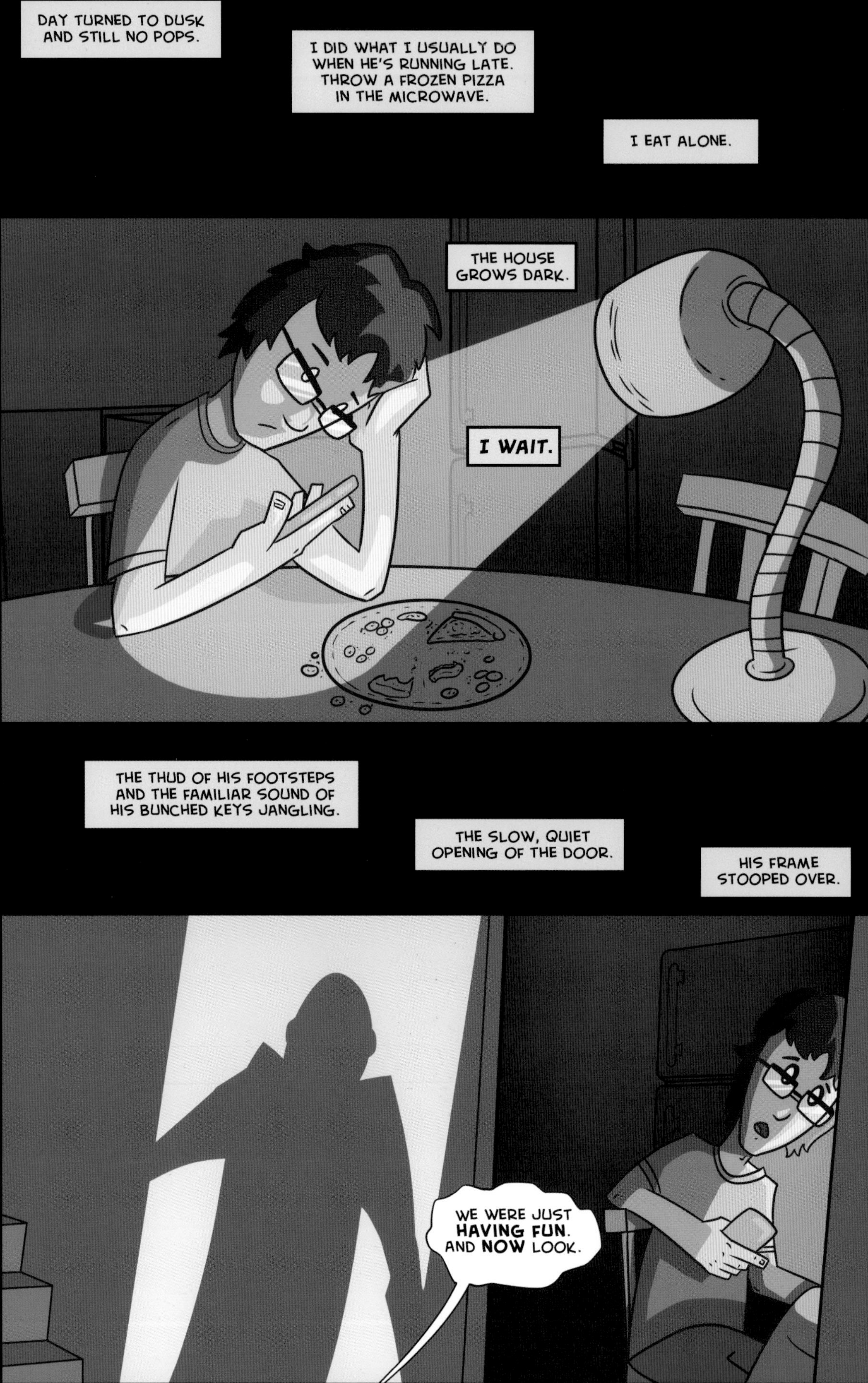
DAY TURNED TO DUSK AND STILL NO POPS.
I DID WHAT I USUALLY DO WHEN HE'S RUNNING LATE. THROW A FROZEN PIZZA IN THE MICROWAVE.
I EAT ALONE.
THE HOUSE GROWS DARK.
I WAIT.
THE THUD OF HIS FOOTSTEPS AND THE FAMILIAR SOUND OF HIS BUNCHED KEYS JANGLING.
THE SLOW, QUIET OPENING OF THE DOOR.
HIS FRAME STOOPED OVER.
WE WERE JUST **HAVING FUN**. AND **NOW** LOOK.

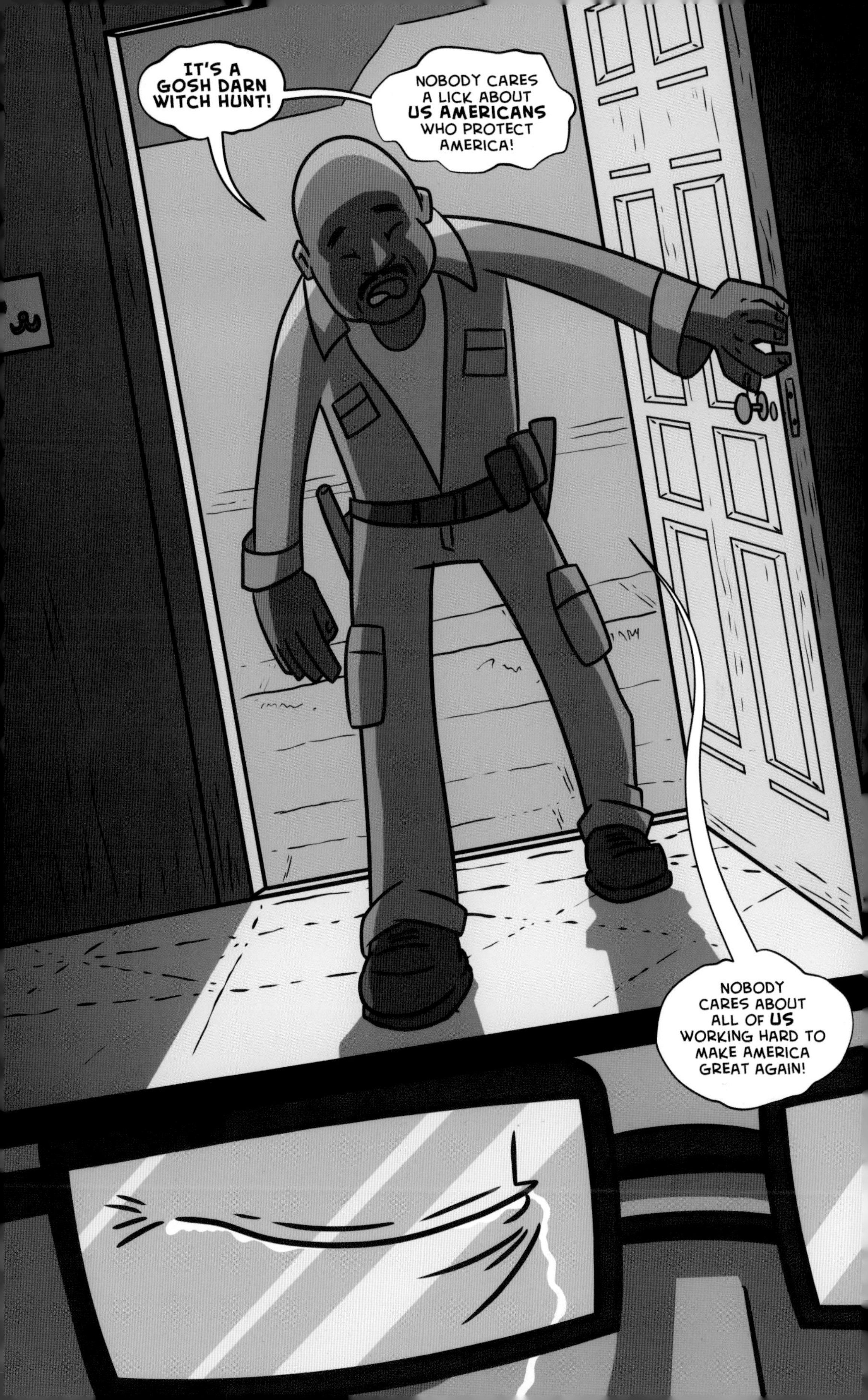
IT'S A GOSH DARN WITCH HUNT!
NOBODY CARES A LICK ABOUT **US AMERICANS** WHO PROTECT AMERICA!
NOBODY CARES ABOUT ALL OF **US** WORKING HARD TO MAKE AMERICA GREAT AGAIN!

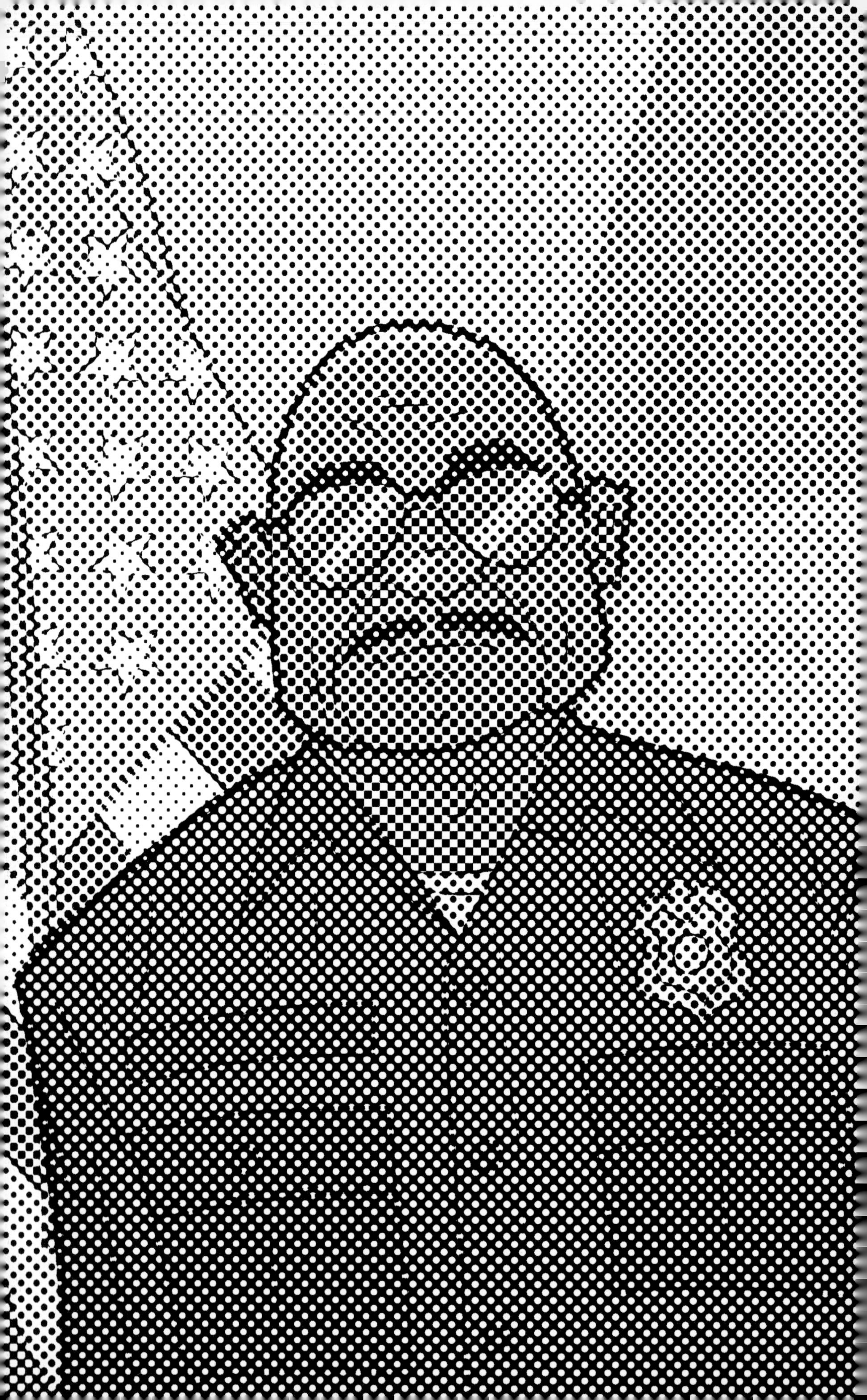

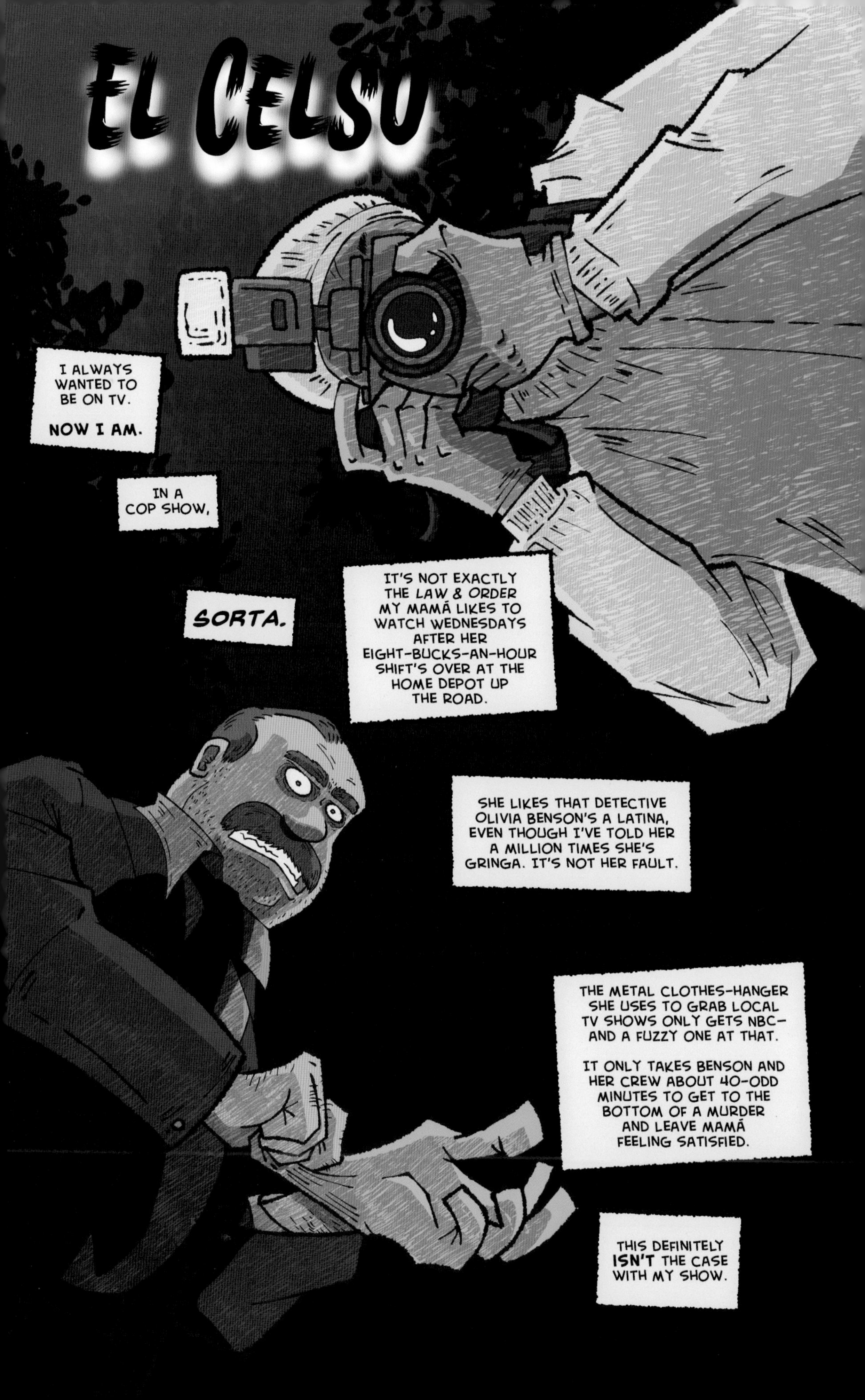

EL CELSO
I ALWAYS WANTED TO BE ON TV.
NOW I AM.
IN A COP SHOW.
SORTA.
IT'S NOT EXACTLY THE LAW & ORDER MY MAMÁ LIKES TO WATCH WEDNESDAYS AFTER HER EIGHT-BUCKS-AN-HOUR SHIFT'S OVER AT THE HOME DEPOT UP THE ROAD.
SHE LIKES THAT DETECTIVE OLIVIA BENSON'S A LATINA, EVEN THOUGH I'VE TOLD HER A MILLION TIMES SHE'S GRINGA. IT'S NOT HER FAULT.
THE METAL CLOTHES-HANGER SHE USES TO GRAB LOCAL TV SHOWS ONLY GETS NBC— AND A FUZZY ONE AT THAT.
IT ONLY TAKES BENSON AND HER CREW ABOUT 40-ODD MINUTES TO GET TO THE BOTTOM OF A MURDER AND LEAVE MAMÁ FEELING SATISFIED.
THIS DEFINITELY ISN'T THE CASE WITH MY SHOW.

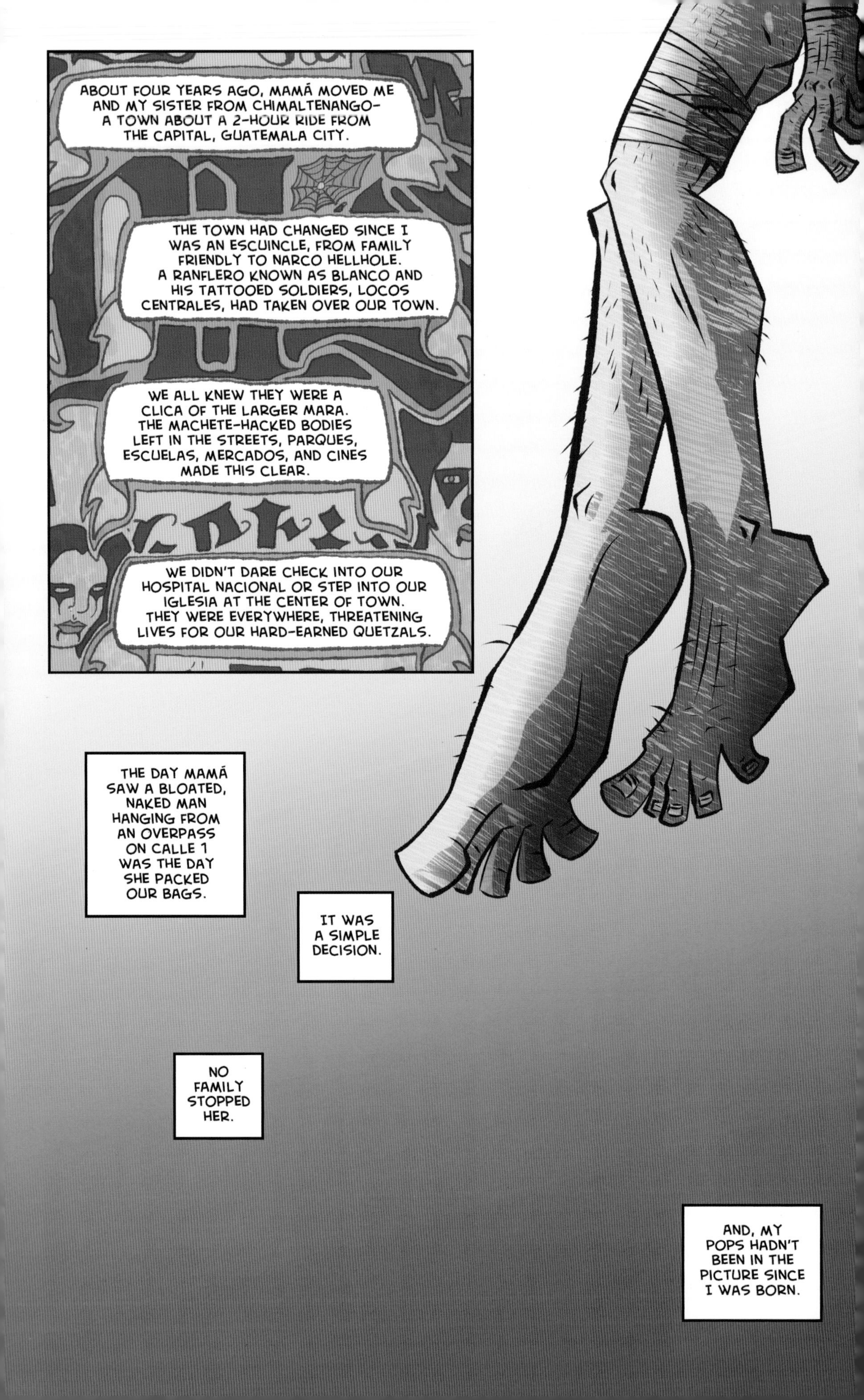
ABOUT FOUR YEARS AGO, MAMÁ MOVED ME AND MY SISTER FROM CHIMALTENANGO– A TOWN ABOUT A 2-HOUR RIDE FROM THE CAPITAL, GUATEMALA CITY.
THE TOWN HAD CHANGED SINCE I WAS AN ESCUINCLE, FROM FAMILY FRIENDLY TO NARCO HELLHOLE. A RANFLERO KNOWN AS BLANCO AND HIS TATTOOED SOLDIERS, LOCOS CENTRALES, HAD TAKEN OVER OUR TOWN.
WE ALL KNEW THEY WERE A CLICA OF THE LARGER MARA. THE MACHETE-HACKED BODIES LEFT IN THE STREETS, PARQUES, ESCUELAS, MERCADOS, AND CINES MADE THIS CLEAR.
WE DIDN'T DARE CHECK INTO OUR HOSPITAL NACIONAL OR STEP INTO OUR IGLESIA AT THE CENTER OF TOWN. THEY WERE EVERYWHERE, THREATENING LIVES FOR OUR HARD-EARNED QUETZALS.
THE DAY MAMÁ SAW A BLOATED, NAKED MAN HANGING FROM AN OVERPASS ON CALLE 1 WAS THE DAY SHE PACKED OUR BAGS.
IT WAS A SIMPLE DECISION.
NO FAMILY STOPPED HER.
AND, MY POPS HADN'T BEEN IN THE PICTURE SINCE I WAS BORN.

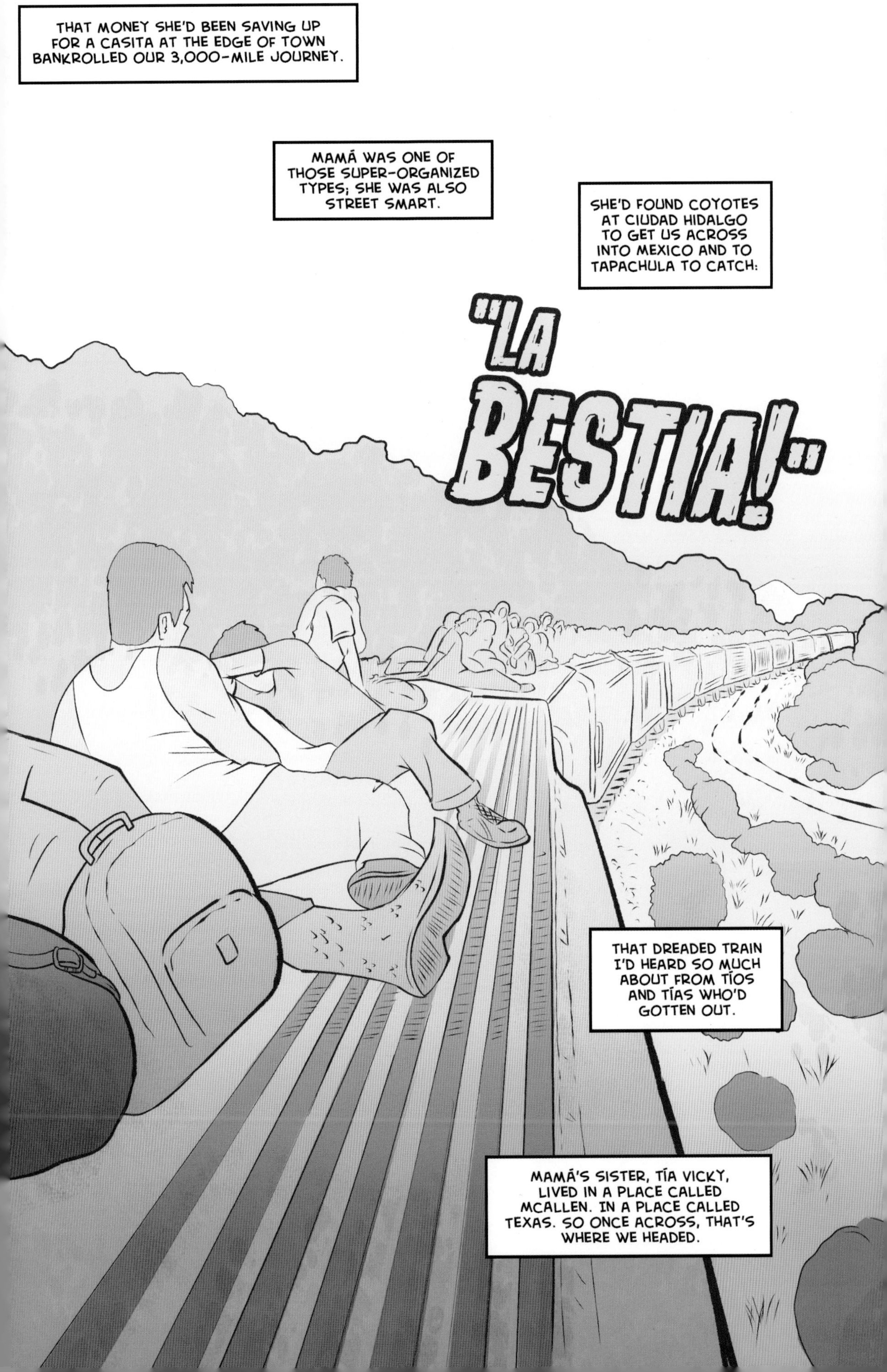
THAT MONEY SHE'D BEEN SAVING UP FOR A CASITA AT THE EDGE OF TOWN BANKROLLED OUR 3,000-MILE JOURNEY.
MAMÁ WAS ONE OF THOSE SUPER-ORGANIZED TYPES; SHE WAS ALSO STREET SMART.
SHE'D FOUND COYOTES AT CIUDAD HIDALGO TO GET US ACROSS INTO MEXICO AND TO TAPACHULA TO CATCH:
"LA BESTIA!"
THAT DREADED TRAIN I'D HEARD SO MUCH ABOUT FROM TÍOS AND TÍAS WHO'D GOTTEN OUT.
MAMÁ'S SISTER, TÍA VICKY, LIVED IN A PLACE CALLED MCALLEN. IN A PLACE CALLED TEXAS. SO ONCE ACROSS, THAT'S WHERE WE HEADED.

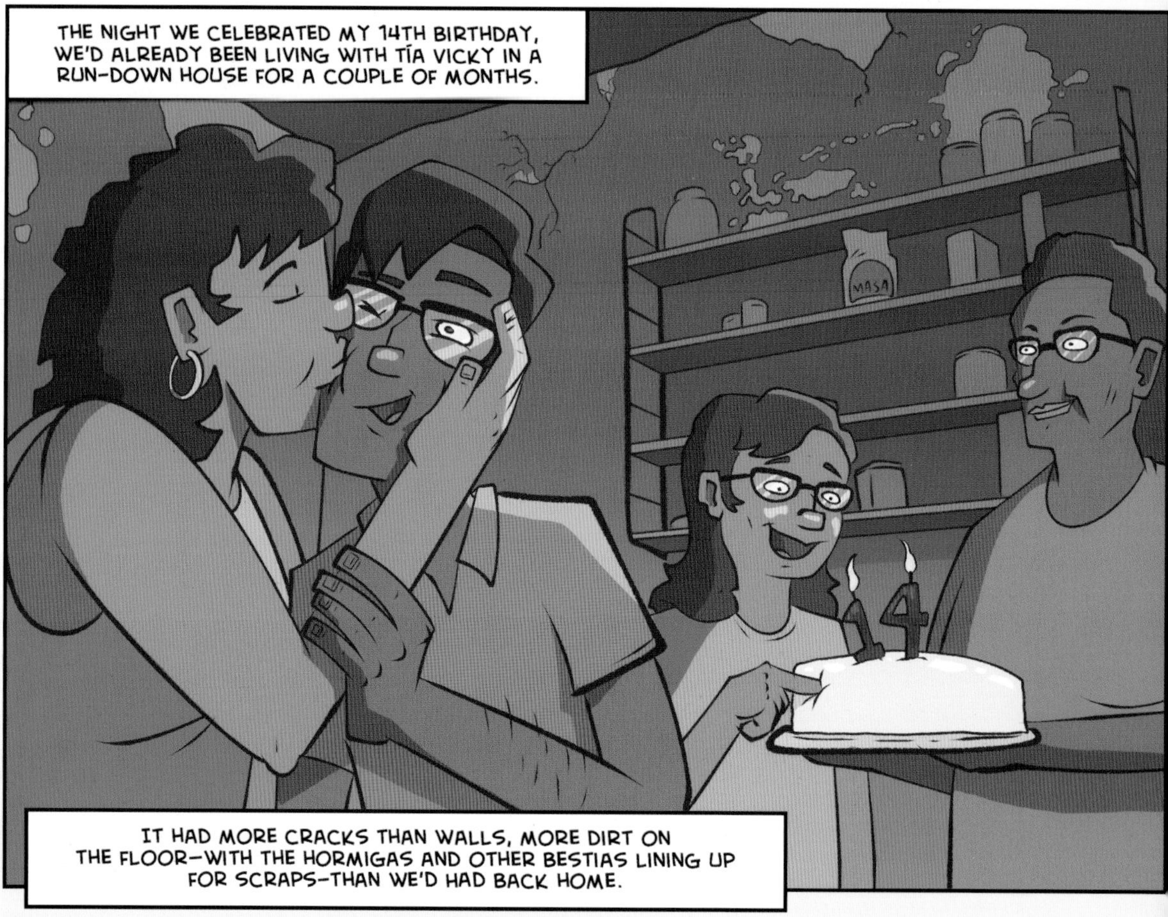
THE NIGHT WE CELEBRATED MY 14TH BIRTHDAY, WE'D ALREADY BEEN LIVING WITH TÍA VICKY IN A RUN-DOWN HOUSE FOR A COUPLE OF MONTHS.
MASA
IT HAD MORE CRACKS THAN WALLS, MORE DIRT ON THE FLOOR—WITH THE HORMIGAS AND OTHER BESTIAS LINING UP FOR SCRAPS—THAN WE'D HAD BACK HOME.

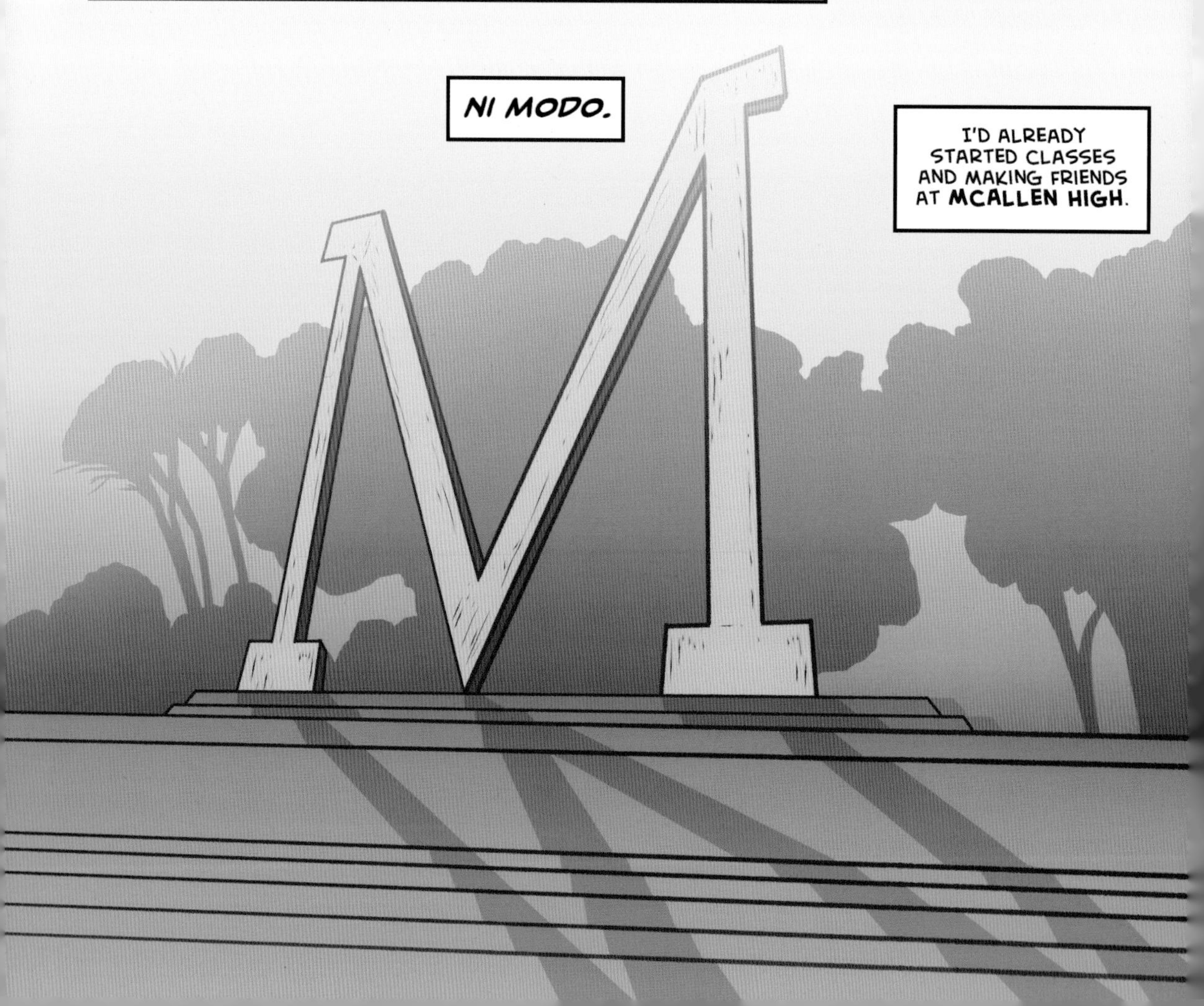
NI MODO.
I'D ALREADY STARTED CLASSES AND MAKING FRIENDS AT MCALLEN HIGH.

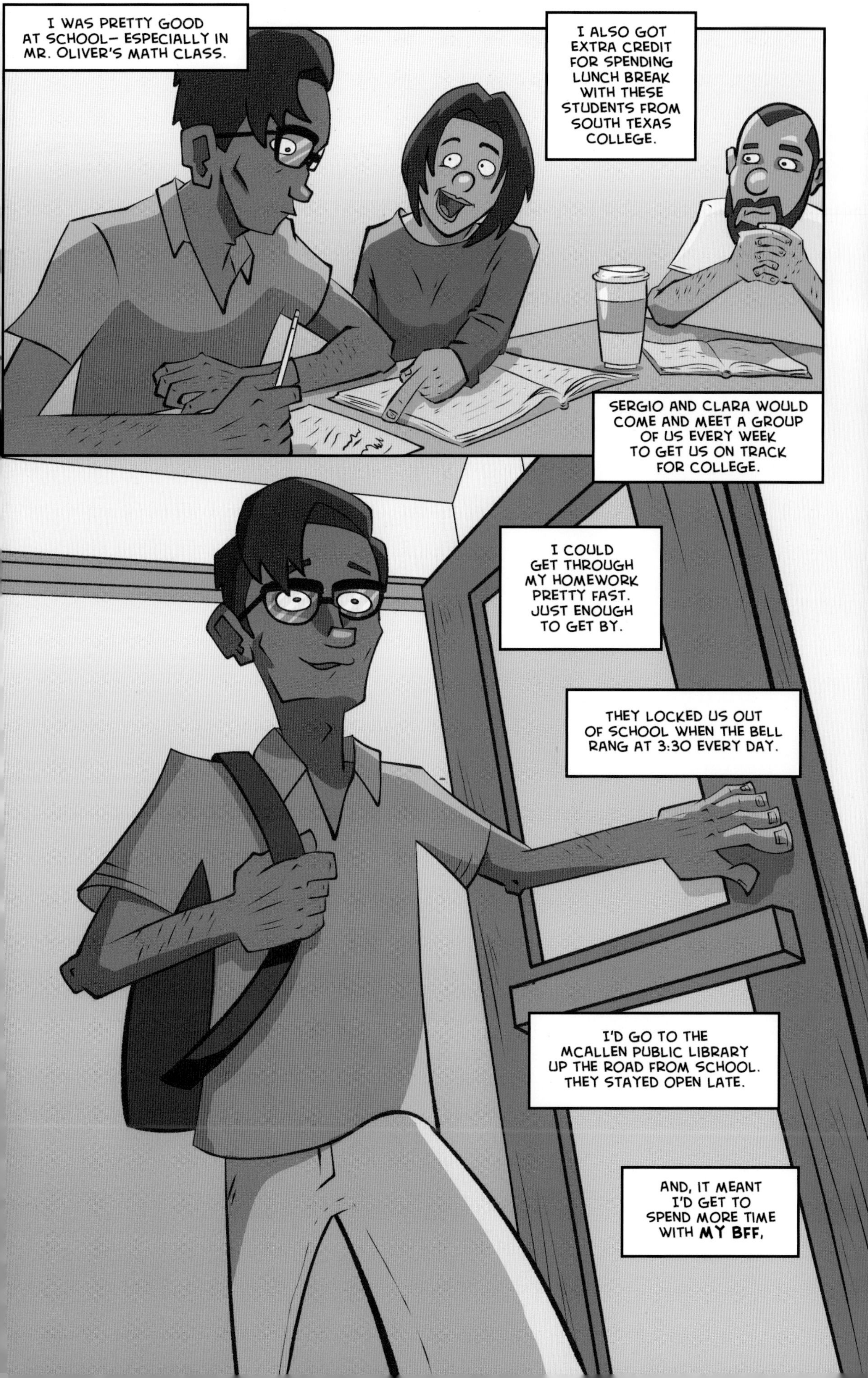
I WAS PRETTY GOOD AT SCHOOL– ESPECIALLY IN MR. OLIVER'S MATH CLASS.
I ALSO GOT EXTRA CREDIT FOR SPENDING LUNCH BREAK WITH THESE STUDENTS FROM SOUTH TEXAS COLLEGE.
SERGIO AND CLARA WOULD COME AND MEET A GROUP OF US EVERY WEEK TO GET US ON TRACK FOR COLLEGE.
I COULD GET THROUGH MY HOMEWORK PRETTY FAST. JUST ENOUGH TO GET BY.
THEY LOCKED US OUT OF SCHOOL WHEN THE BELL RANG AT 3:30 EVERY DAY.
I'D GO TO THE MCALLEN PUBLIC LIBRARY UP THE ROAD FROM SCHOOL. THEY STAYED OPEN LATE.
AND, IT MEANT I'D GET TO SPEND MORE TIME WITH **MY BFF**.

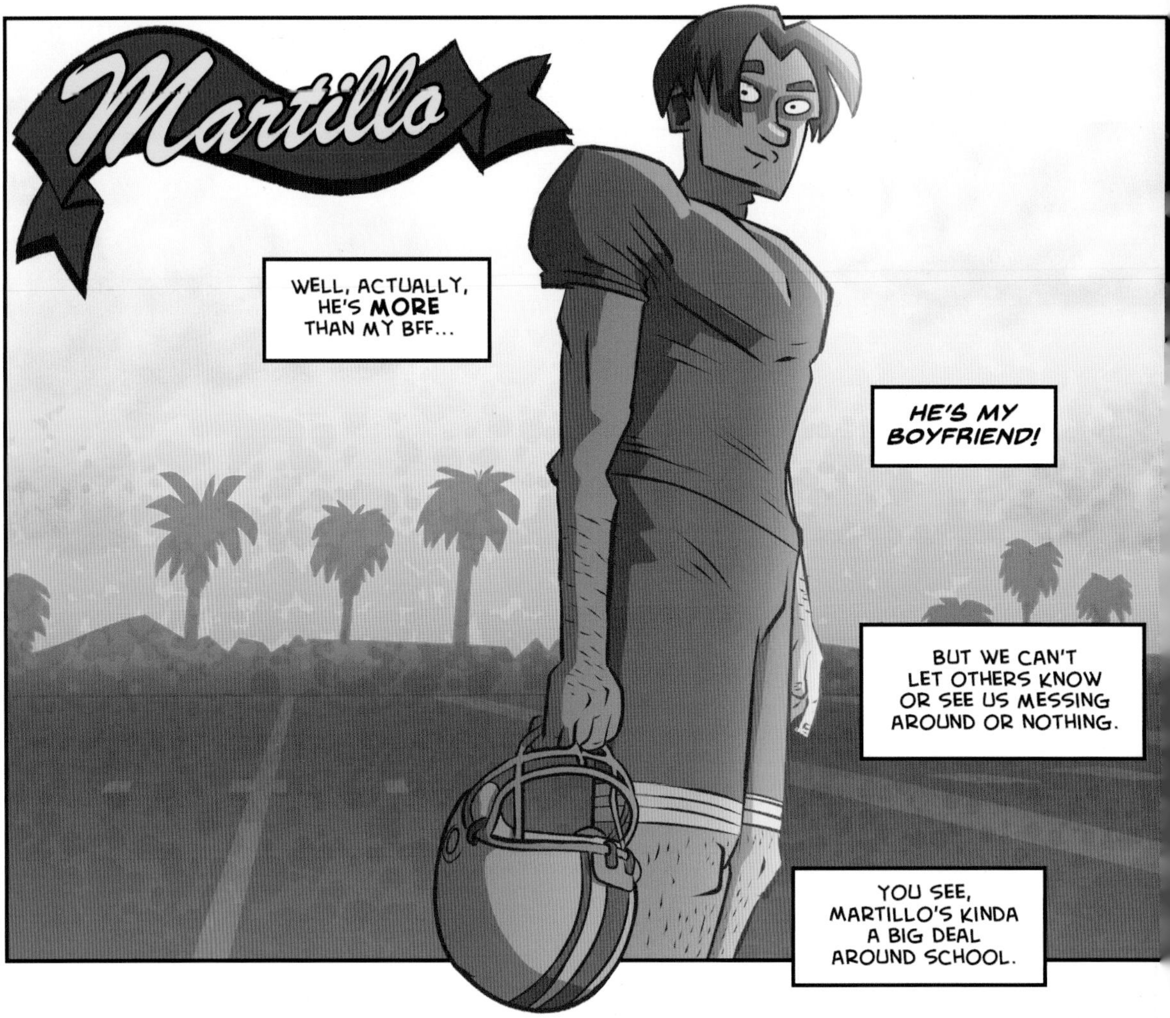
Martillo
WELL, ACTUALLY, HE'S MORE THAN MY BFF...
HE'S MY BOYFRIEND!
BUT WE CAN'T LET OTHERS KNOW OR SEE US MESSING AROUND OR NOTHING.
YOU SEE, MARTILLO'S KINDA A BIG DEAL AROUND SCHOOL.

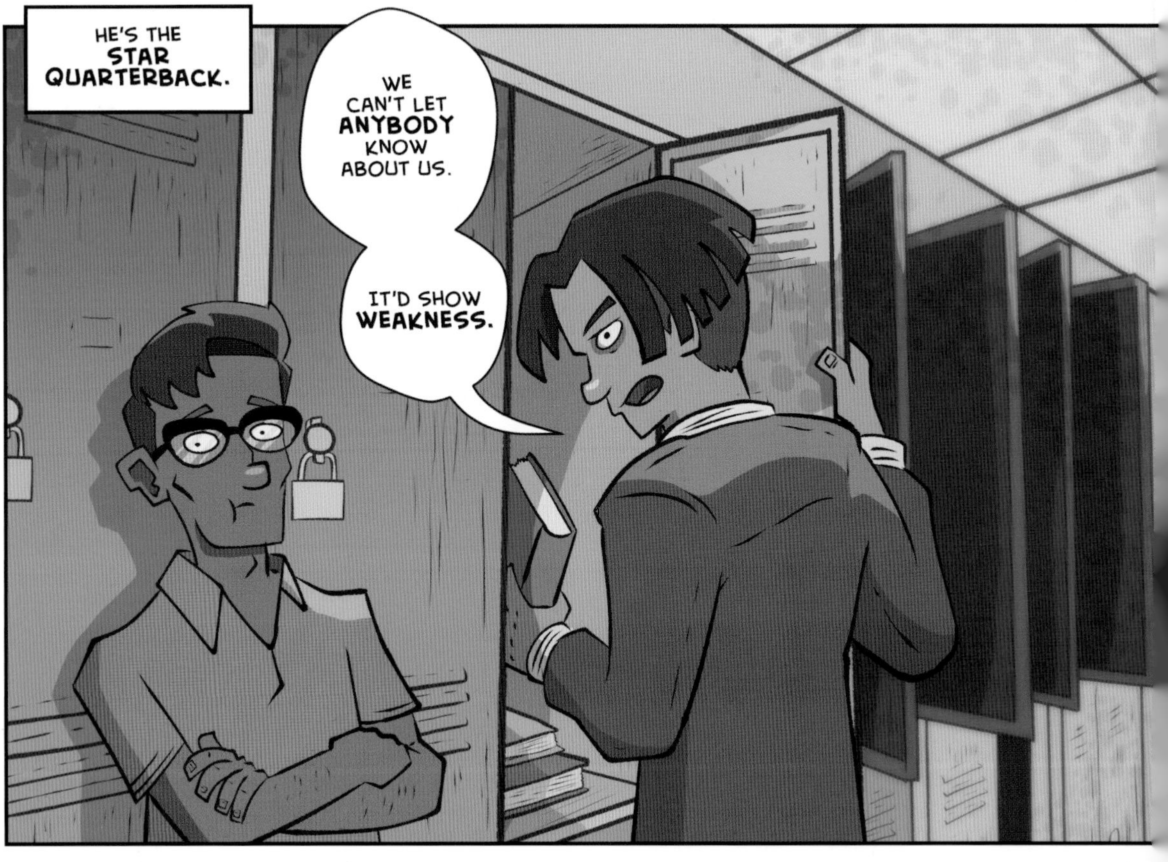
HE'S THE STAR QUARTERBACK.
WE CAN'T LET ANYBODY KNOW ABOUT US.
IT'D SHOW WEAKNESS.

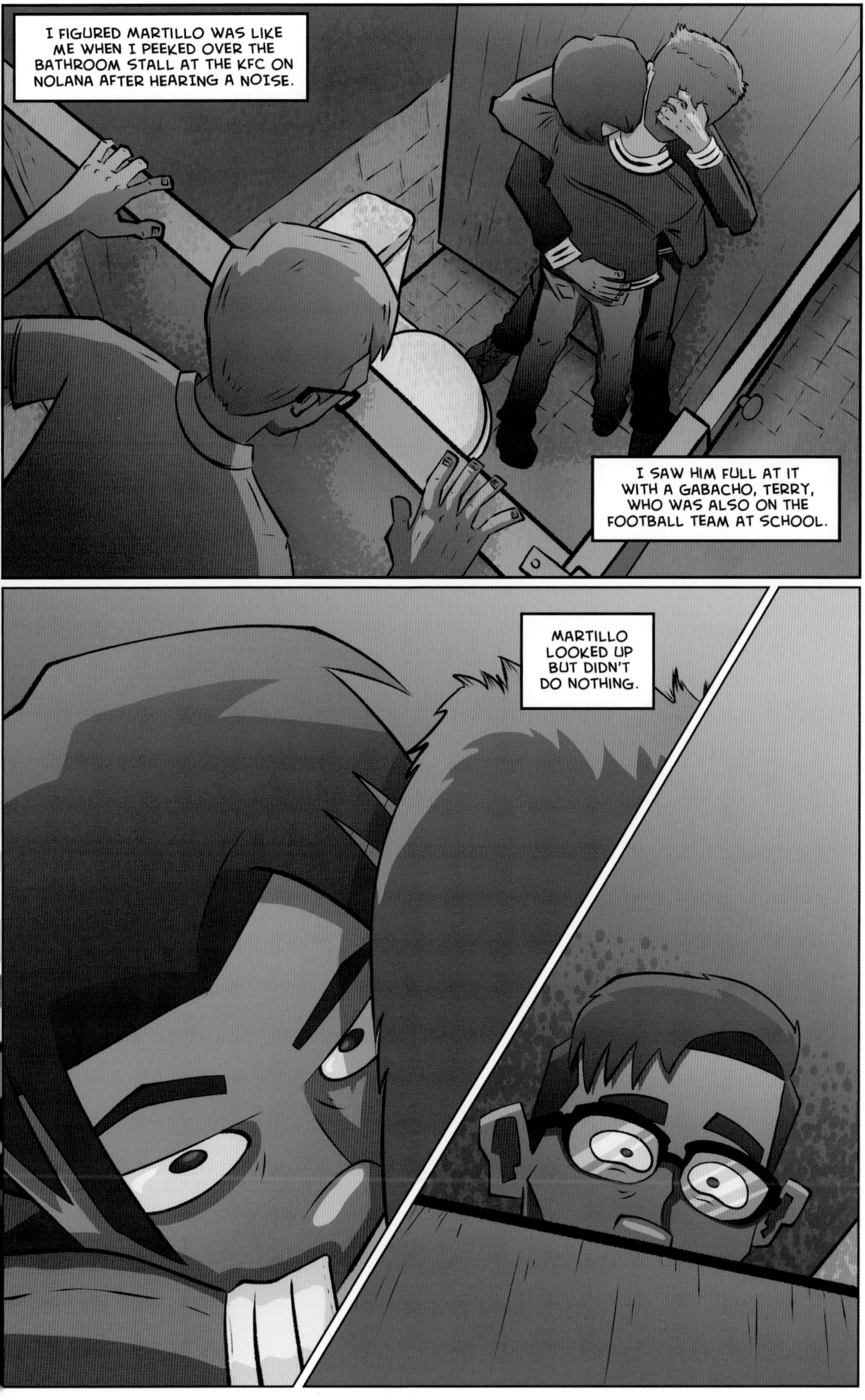
I FIGURED MARTILLO WAS LIKE ME WHEN I PEEKED OVER THE BATHROOM STALL AT THE KFC ON NOLANA AFTER HEARING A NOISE.
I SAW HIM FULL AT IT WITH A GABACHO, TERRY, WHO WAS ALSO ON THE FOOTBALL TEAM AT SCHOOL.
MARTILLO LOOKED UP BUT DIDN'T DO NOTHING.

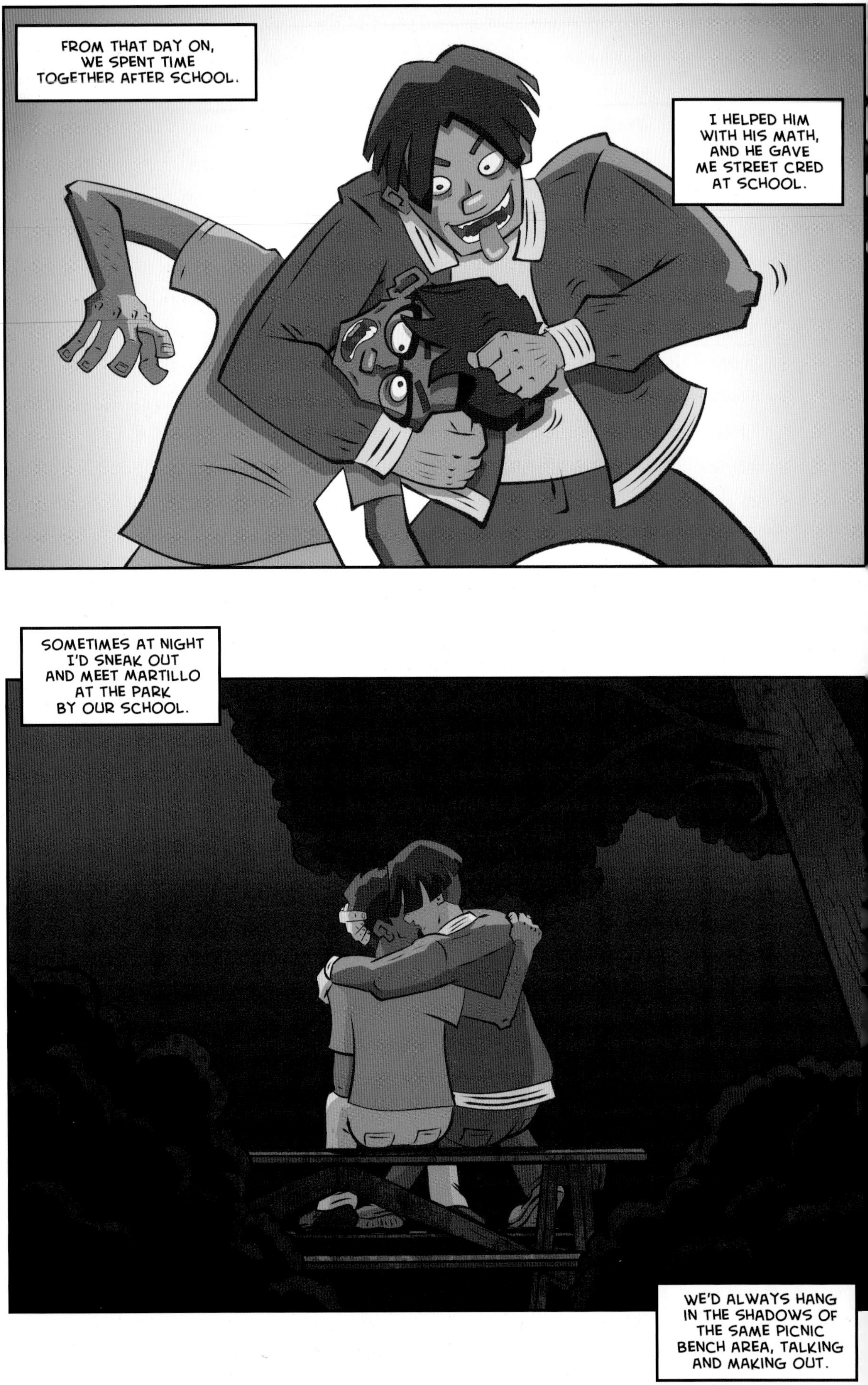
FROM THAT DAY ON, WE SPENT TIME TOGETHER AFTER SCHOOL.
I HELPED HIM WITH HIS MATH, AND HE GAVE ME STREET CRED AT SCHOOL.
SOMETIMES AT NIGHT I'D SNEAK OUT AND MEET MARTILLO AT THE PARK BY OUR SCHOOL.
WE'D ALWAYS HANG IN THE SHADOWS OF THE SAME PICNIC BENCH AREA, TALKING AND MAKING OUT.

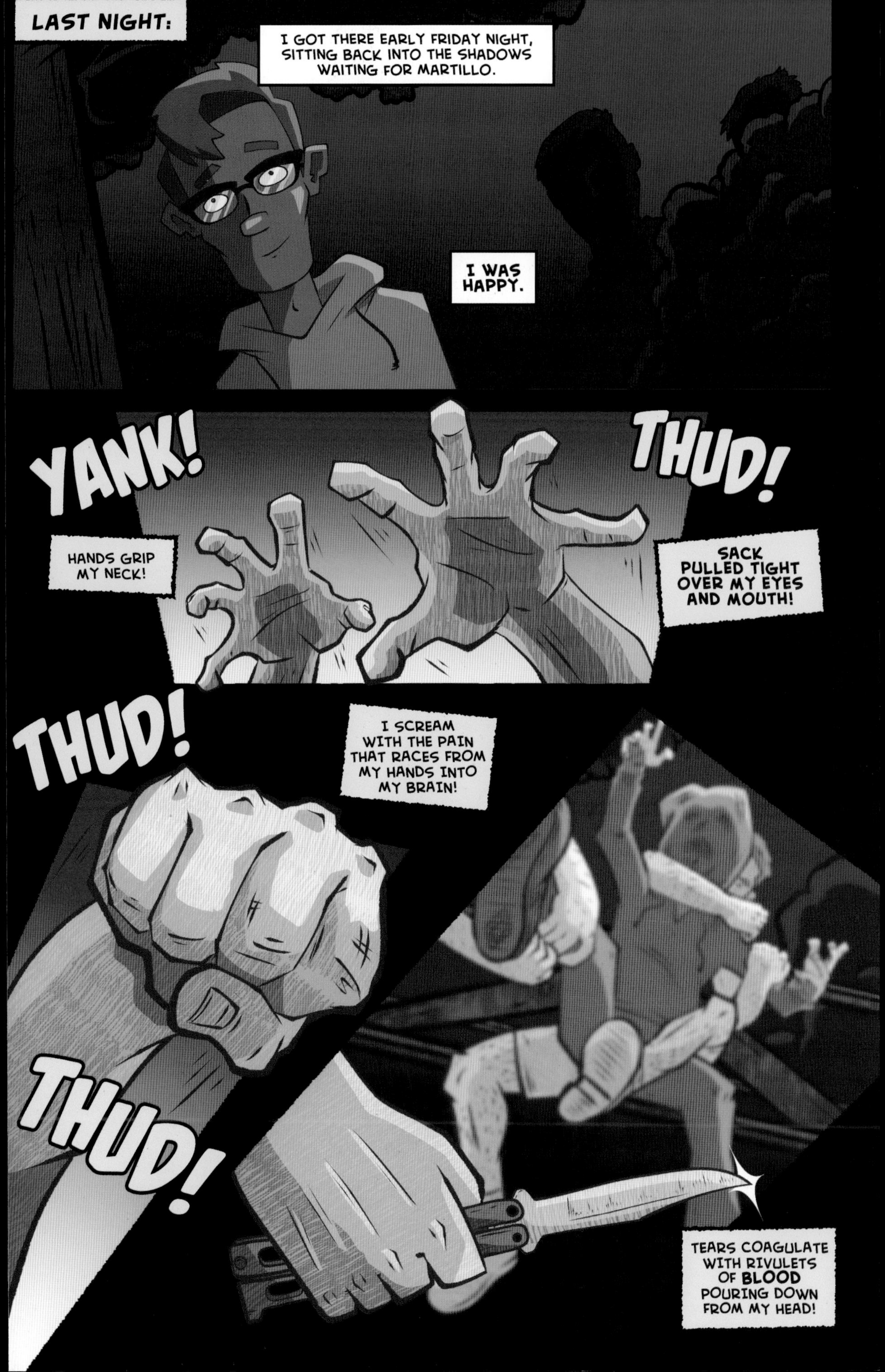

LAST NIGHT:
I GOT THERE EARLY FRIDAY NIGHT, SITTING BACK INTO THE SHADOWS WAITING FOR MARTILLO.
I WAS HAPPY.
YANK!
HANDS GRIP MY NECK!
THUD!
SACK PULLED TIGHT OVER MY EYES AND MOUTH!
THUD!
I SCREAM WITH THE PAIN THAT RACES FROM MY HANDS INTO MY BRAIN!
THUD!
TEARS COAGULATE WITH RIVULETS OF BLOOD POURING DOWN FROM MY HEAD!

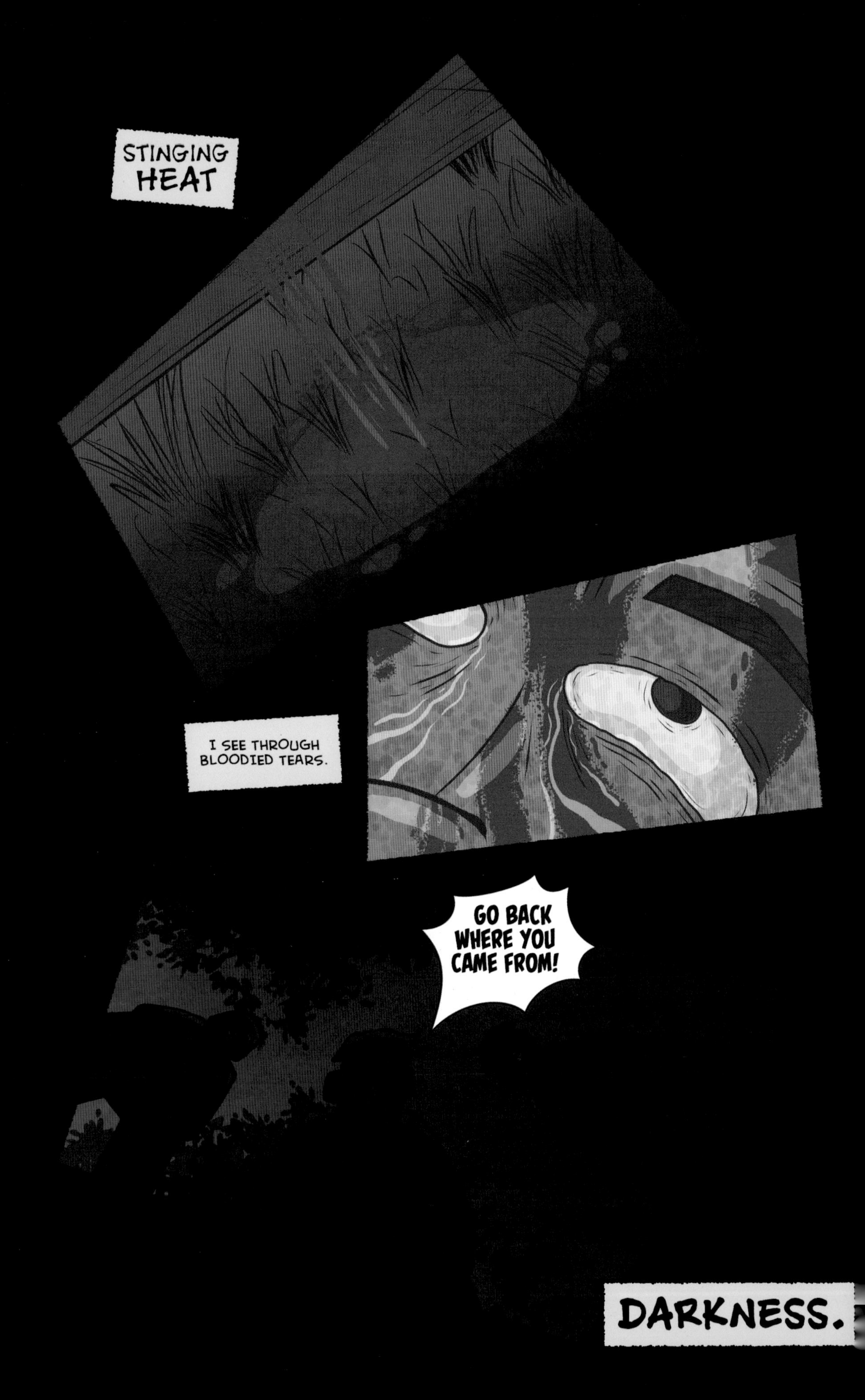
STINGING HEAT
I SEE THROUGH BLOODIED TEARS.
GO BACK WHERE YOU CAME FROM!
DARKNESS.

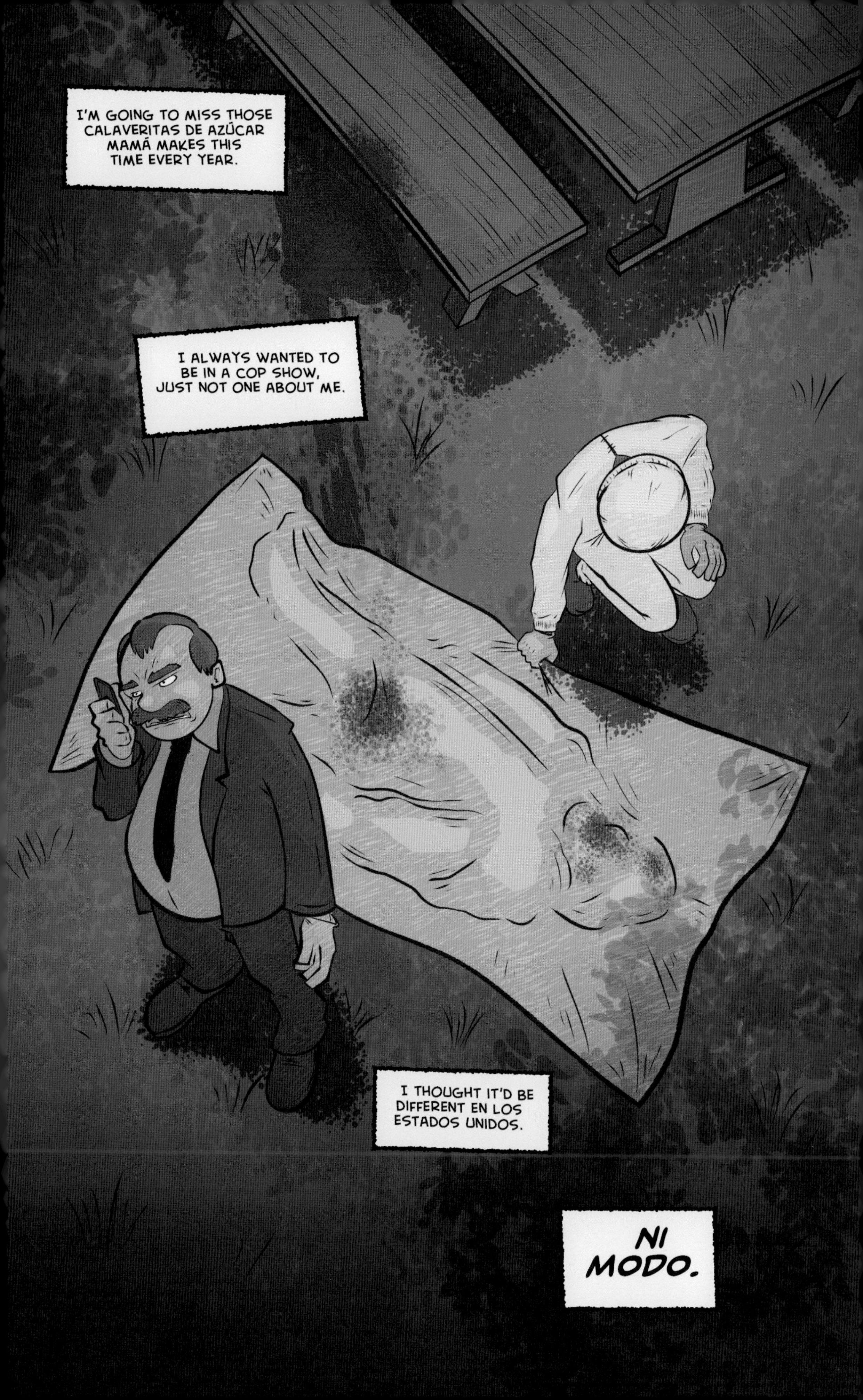
I'M GOING TO MISS THOSE CALAVERITAS DE AZÚCAR MAMÁ MAKES THIS TIME EVERY YEAR.
I ALWAYS WANTED TO BE IN A COP SHOW, JUST NOT ONE ABOUT ME.
I THOUGHT IT'D BE DIFFERENT EN LOS ESTADOS UNIDOS.
NI MODO.

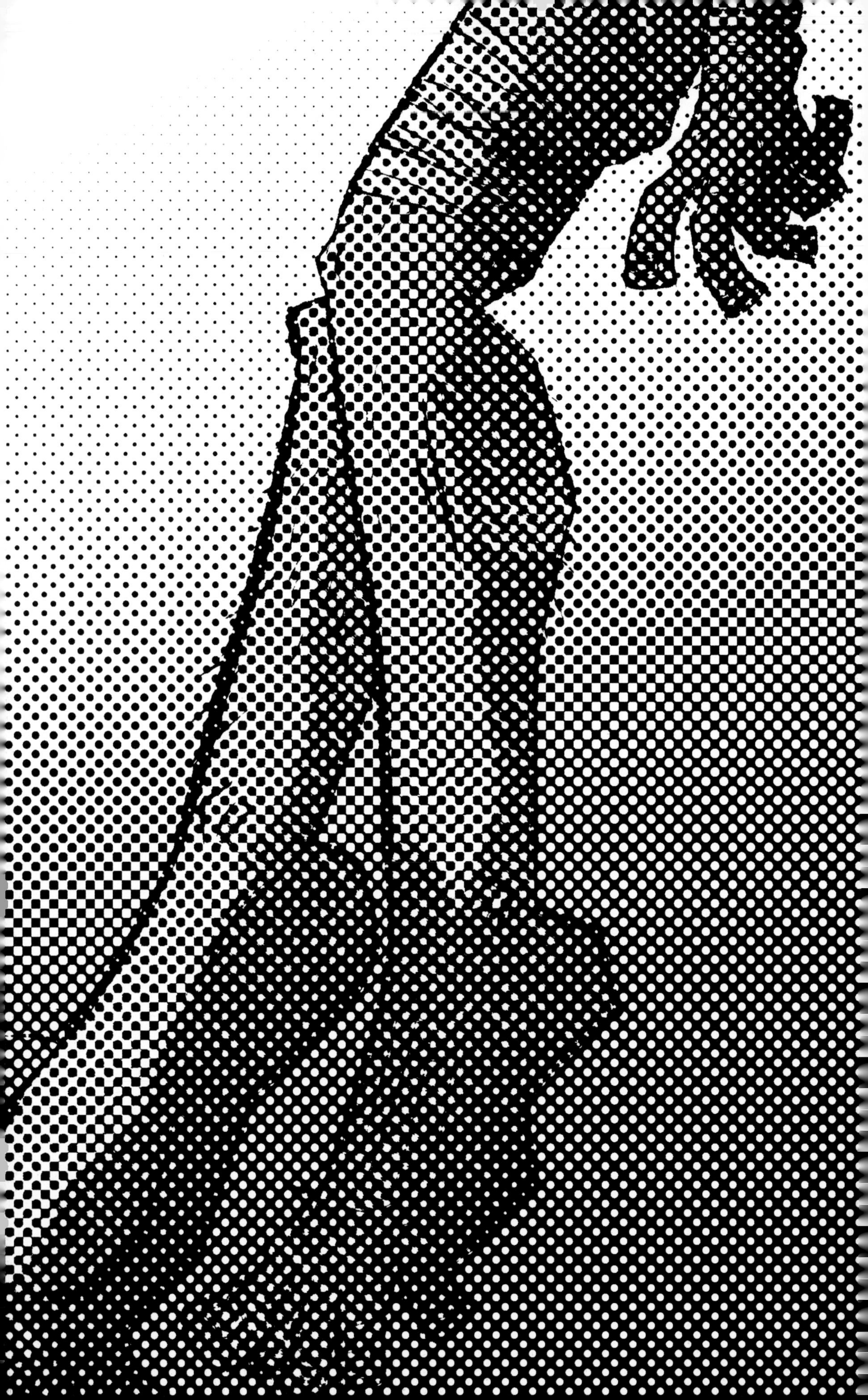

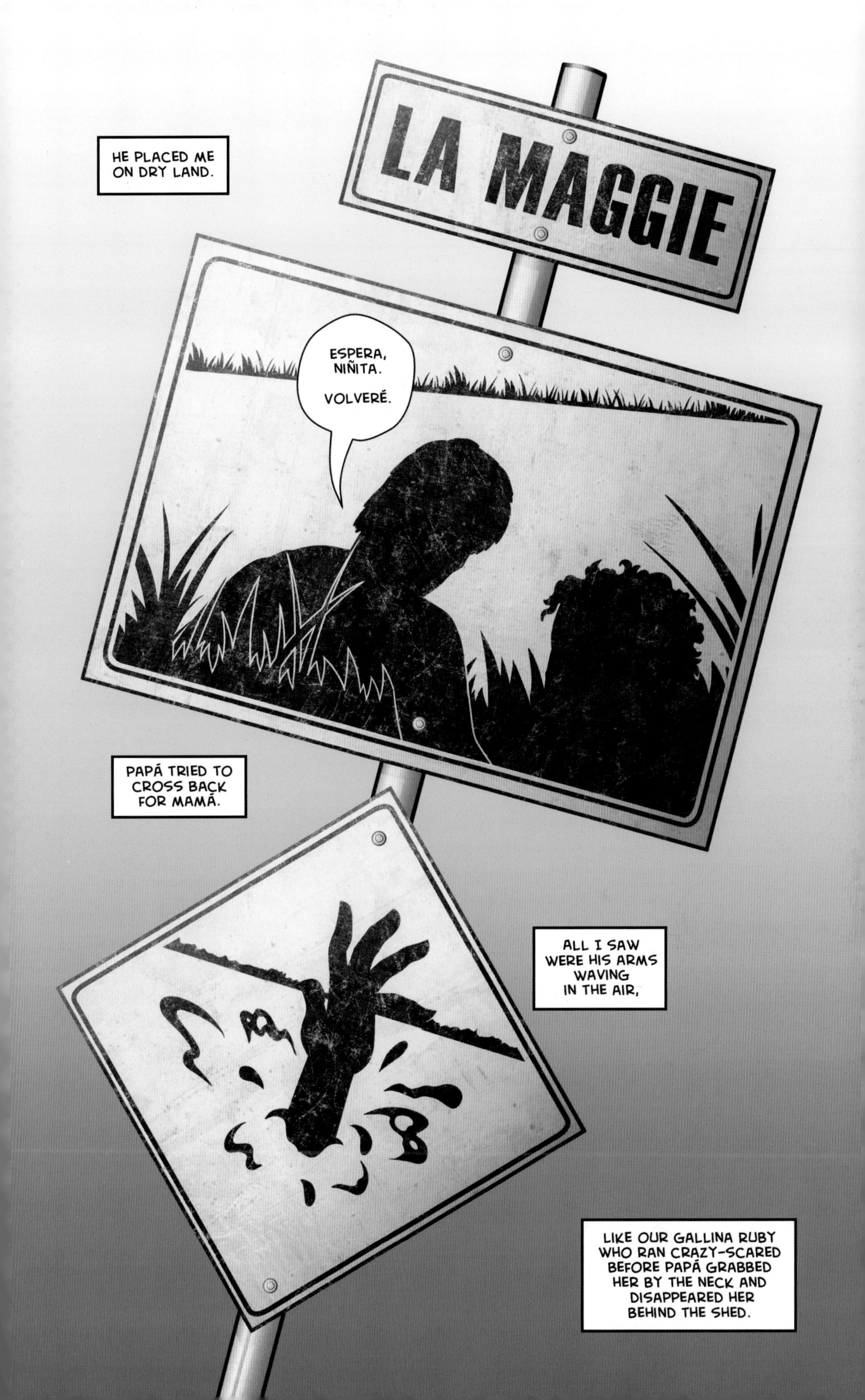
HE PLACED ME ON DRY LAND.
LA MAGGIE
ESPERA, NIÑITA. VOLVERÉ.
PAPÁ TRIED TO CROSS BACK FOR MAMÁ.
ALL I SAW WERE HIS ARMS WAVING IN THE AIR,
LIKE OUR GALLINA RUBY WHO RAN CRAZY-SCARED BEFORE PAPÁ GRABBED HER BY THE NECK AND DISAPPEARED HER BEHIND THE SHED.

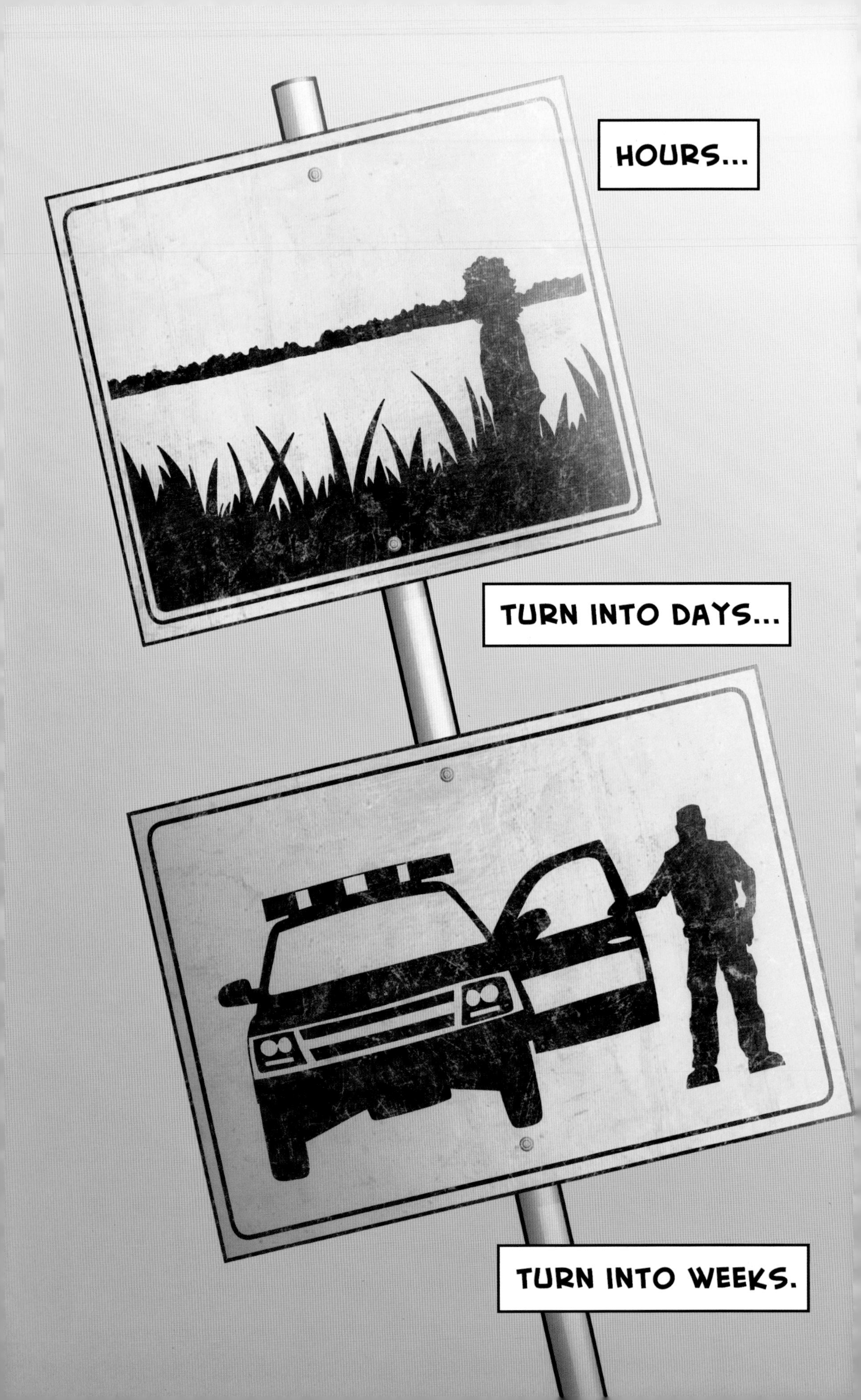
HOURS...
TURN INTO DAYS...
TURN INTO WEEKS.

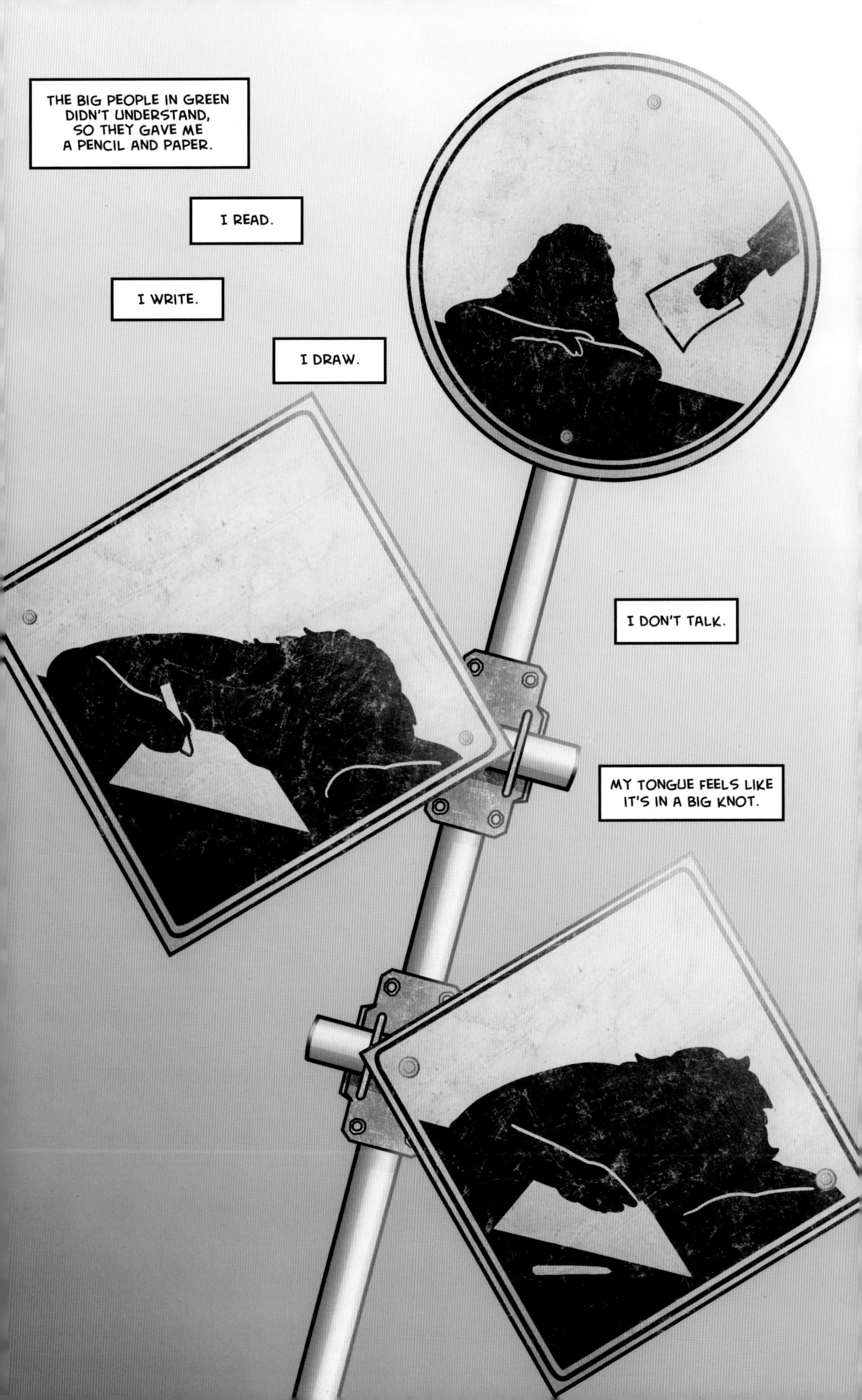
THE BIG PEOPLE IN GREEN DIDN'T UNDERSTAND, SO THEY GAVE ME A PENCIL AND PAPER.
I READ.
I WRITE.
I DRAW.
I DON'T TALK.
MY TONGUE FEELS LIKE IT'S IN A BIG KNOT.

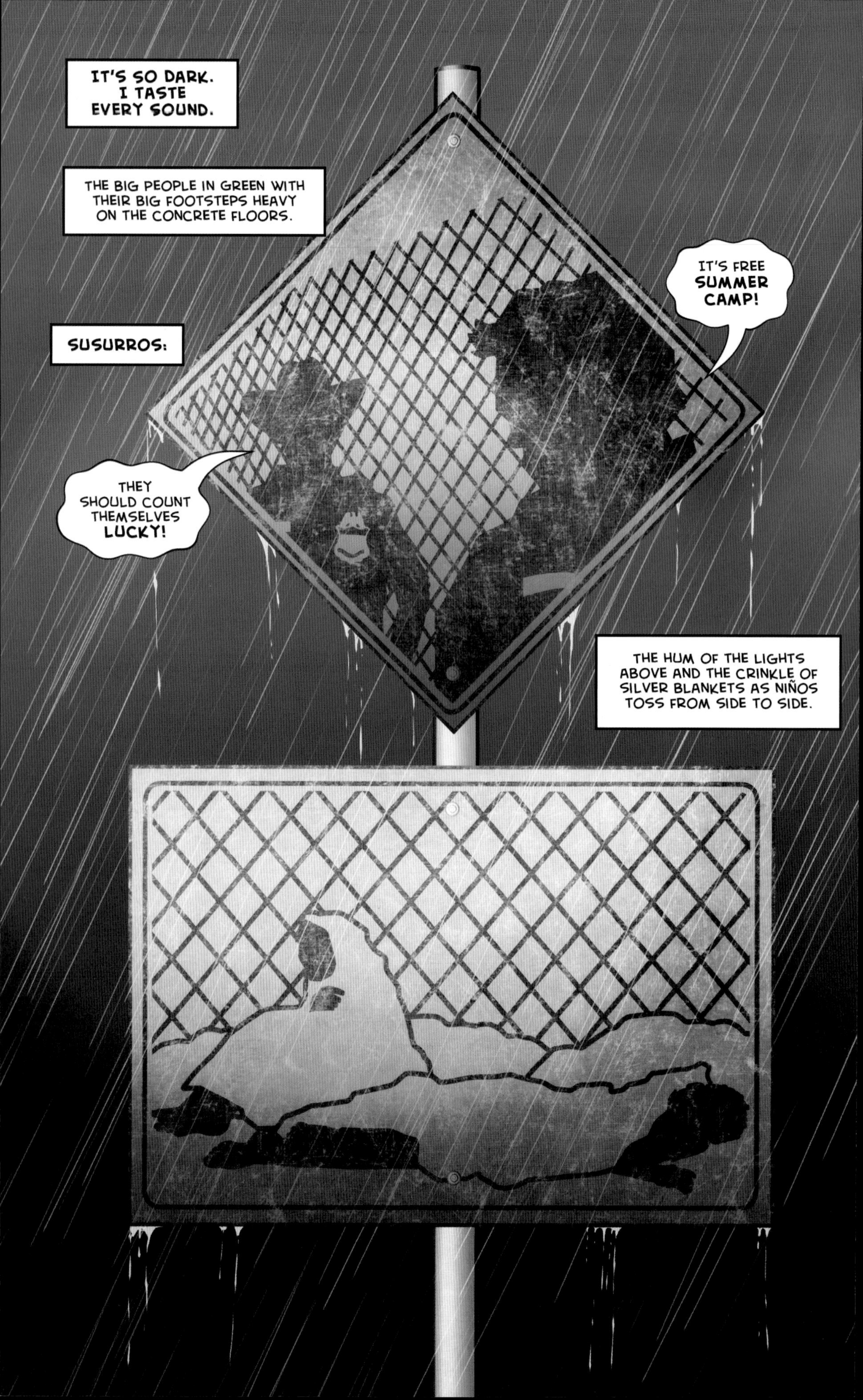
IT'S SO DARK. I TASTE EVERY SOUND.
THE BIG PEOPLE IN GREEN WITH THEIR BIG FOOTSTEPS HEAVY ON THE CONCRETE FLOORS.
SUSURROS:
IT'S FREE SUMMER CAMP!
THEY SHOULD COUNT THEMSELVES LUCKY!
THE HUM OF THE LIGHTS ABOVE AND THE CRINKLE OF SILVER BLANKETS AS NIÑOS TOSS FROM SIDE TO SIDE.

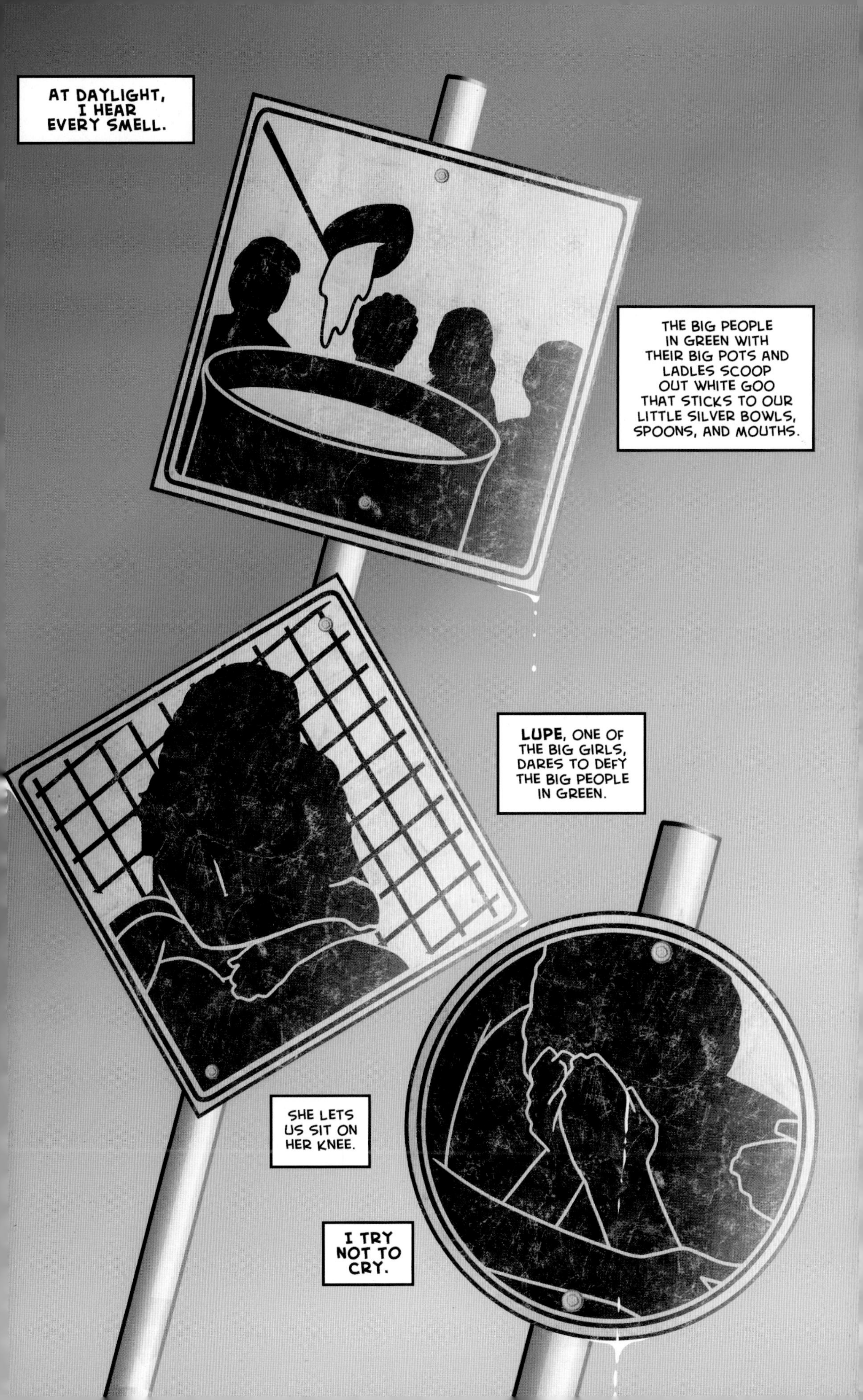
AT DAYLIGHT, I HEAR EVERY SMELL.
THE BIG PEOPLE IN GREEN WITH THEIR BIG POTS AND LADLES SCOOP OUT WHITE GOO THAT STICKS TO OUR LITTLE SILVER BOWLS, SPOONS, AND MOUTHS.
LUPE, ONE OF THE BIG GIRLS, DARES TO DEFY THE BIG PEOPLE IN GREEN.
SHE LETS US SIT ON HER KNEE.
I TRY NOT TO CRY.

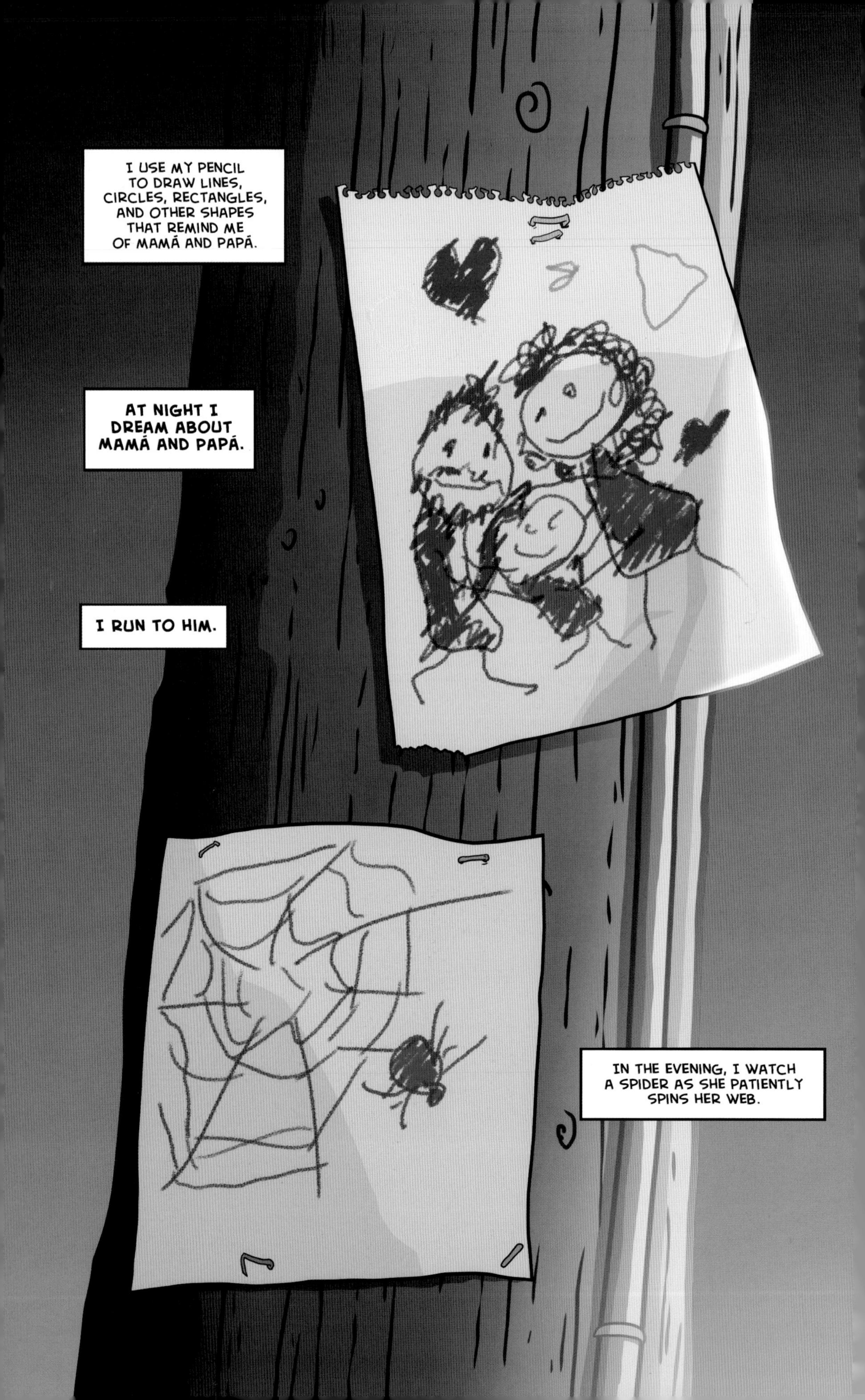
I USE MY PENCIL TO DRAW LINES, CIRCLES, RECTANGLES, AND OTHER SHAPES THAT REMIND ME OF MAMÁ AND PAPÁ.
AT NIGHT I DREAM ABOUT MAMÁ AND PAPÁ.
I RUN TO HIM.
IN THE EVENING, I WATCH A SPIDER AS SHE PATIENTLY SPINS HER WEB.

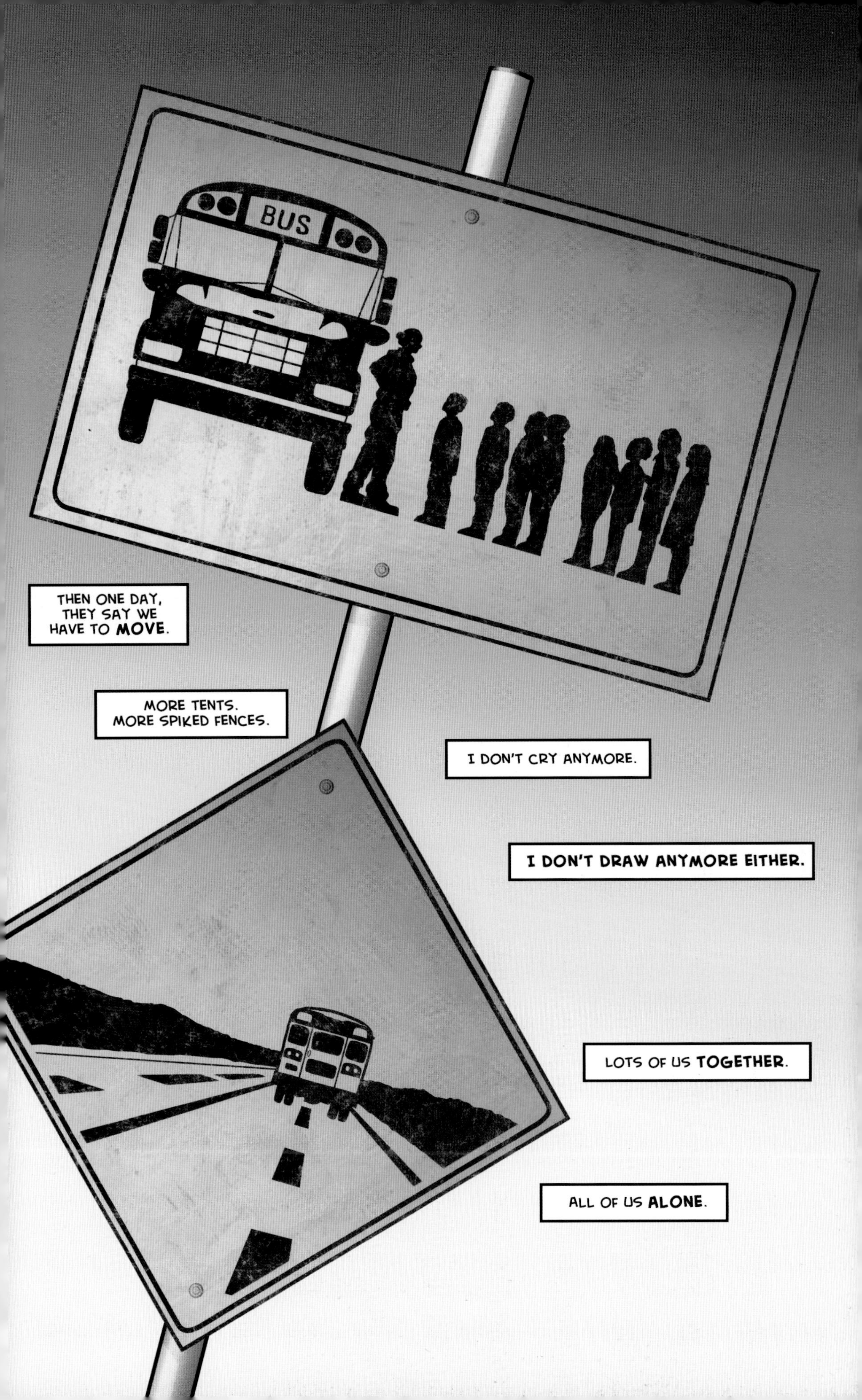

BUS
THEN ONE DAY, THEY SAY WE HAVE TO **MOVE**.
MORE TENTS. MORE SPIKED FENCES.
I DON'T CRY ANYMORE.
I DON'T DRAW ANYMORE EITHER.
LOTS OF US **TOGETHER**.
ALL OF US **ALONE**.

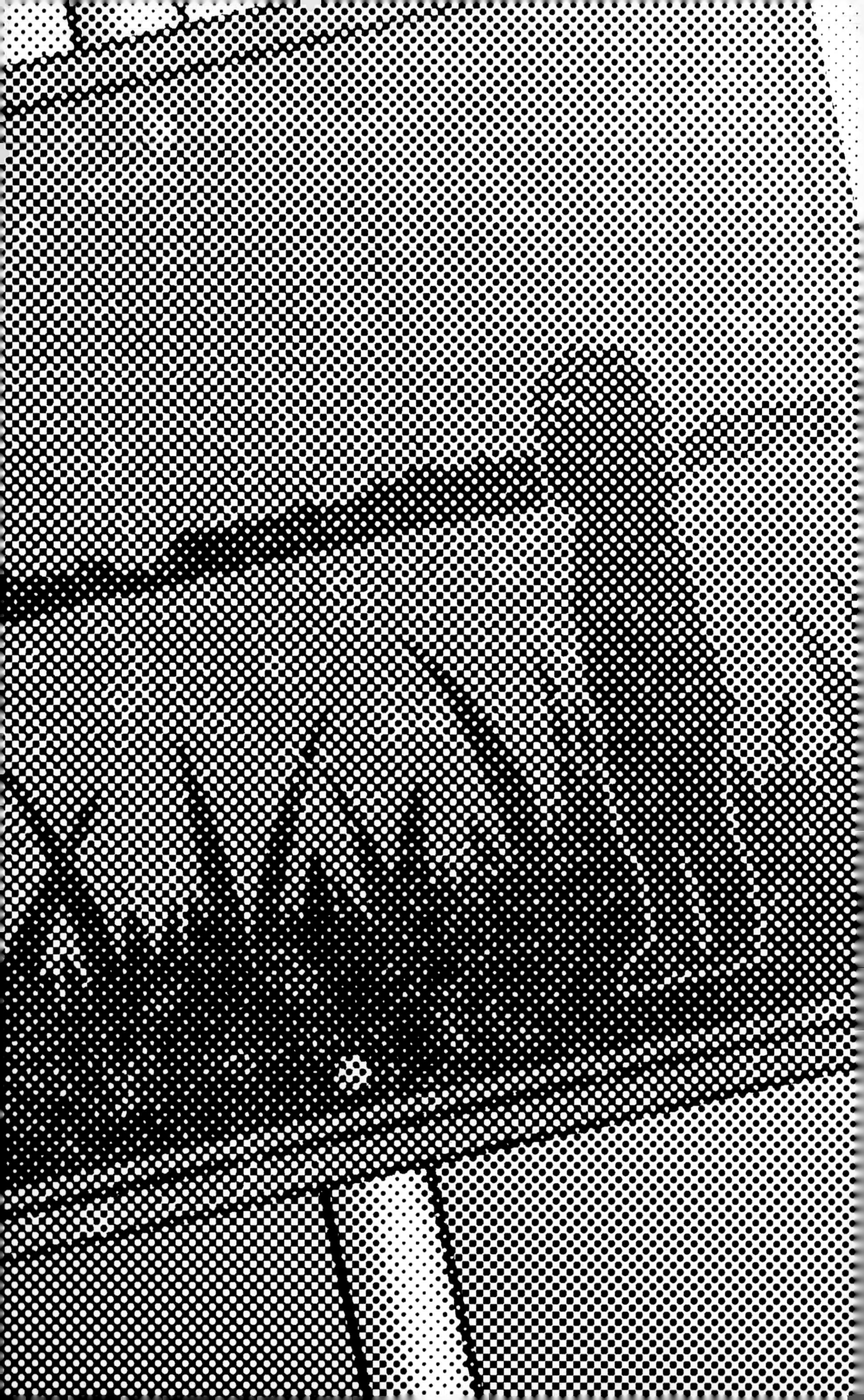

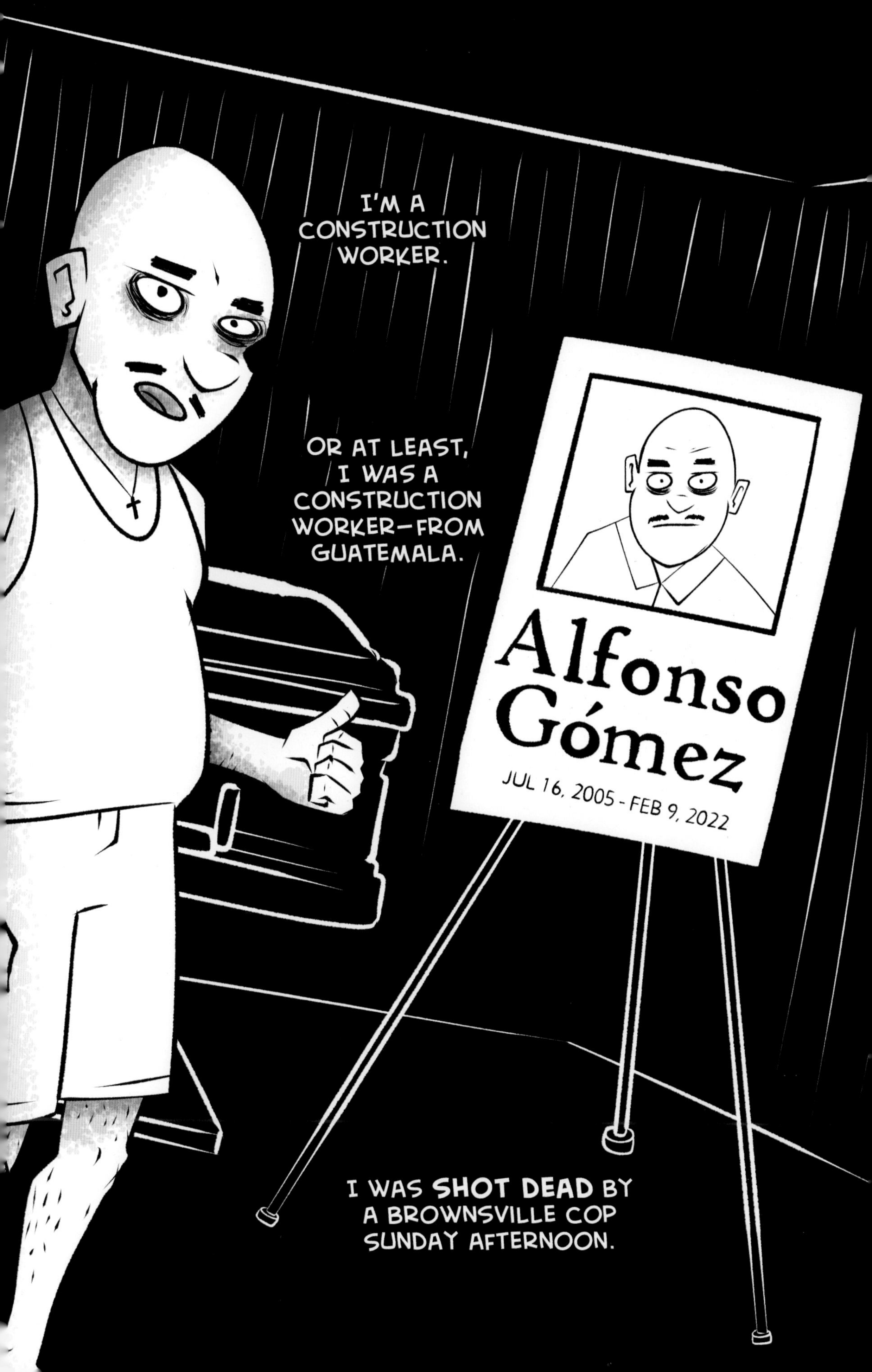
I'M A CONSTRUCTION WORKER.
OR AT LEAST, I WAS A CONSTRUCTION WORKER—FROM GUATEMALA.
Alfonso Gómez
JUL 16, 2005 - FEB 9, 2022
I WAS **SHOT DEAD** BY A BROWNSVILLE COP SUNDAY AFTERNOON.

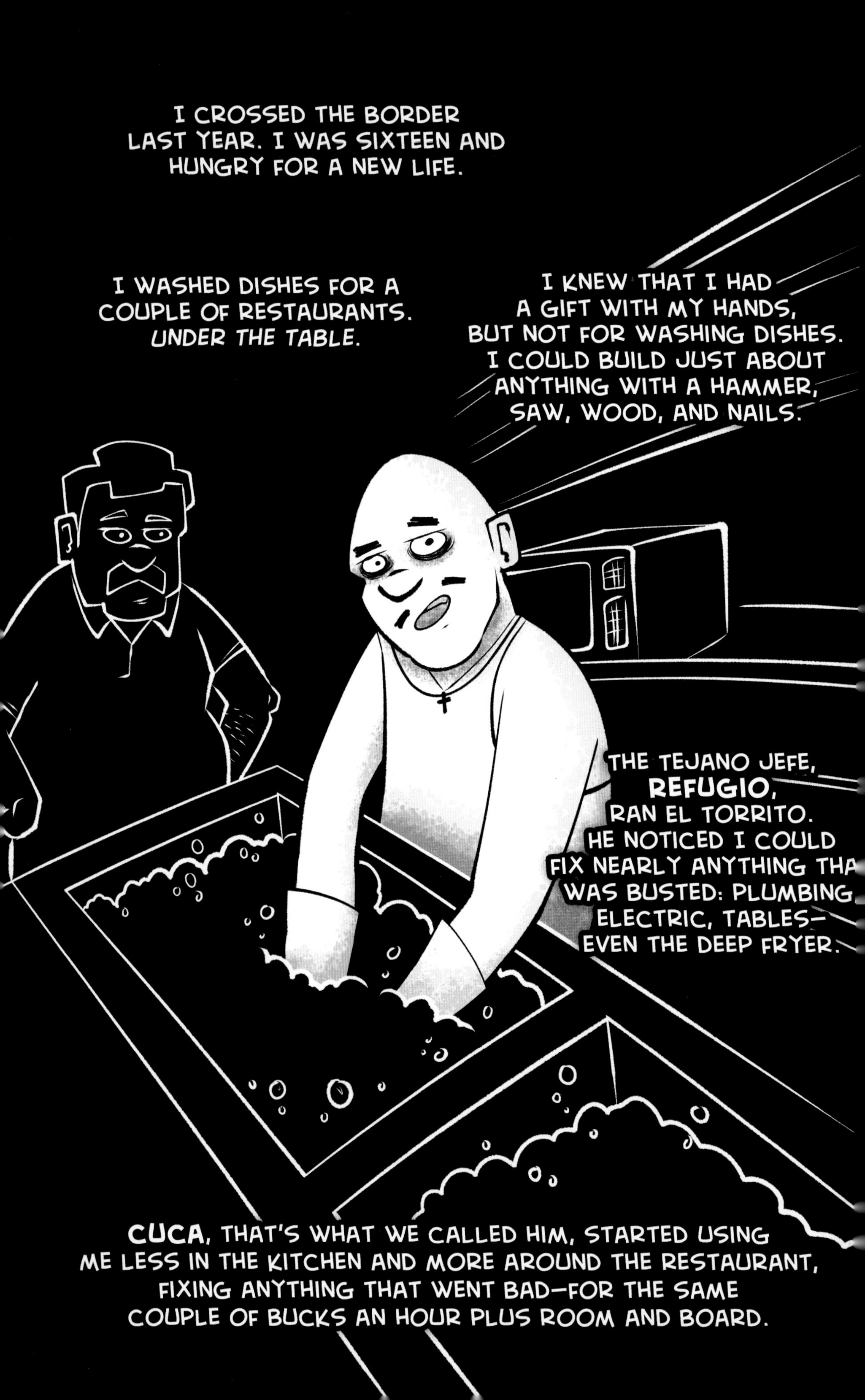
I CROSSED THE BORDER LAST YEAR. I WAS SIXTEEN AND HUNGRY FOR A NEW LIFE.
I WASHED DISHES FOR A COUPLE OF RESTAURANTS. UNDER THE TABLE.
I KNEW THAT I HAD A GIFT WITH MY HANDS, BUT NOT FOR WASHING DISHES. I COULD BUILD JUST ABOUT ANYTHING WITH A HAMMER, SAW, WOOD, AND NAILS.
THE TEJANO JEFE, REFUGIO, RAN EL TORRITO. HE NOTICED I COULD FIX NEARLY ANYTHING THA WAS BUSTED: PLUMBING, ELECTRIC, TABLES—EVEN THE DEEP FRYER.
CUCA, THAT'S WHAT WE CALLED HIM, STARTED USING ME LESS IN THE KITCHEN AND MORE AROUND THE RESTAURANT, FIXING ANYTHING THAT WENT BAD—FOR THE SAME COUPLE OF BUCKS AN HOUR PLUS ROOM AND BOARD.

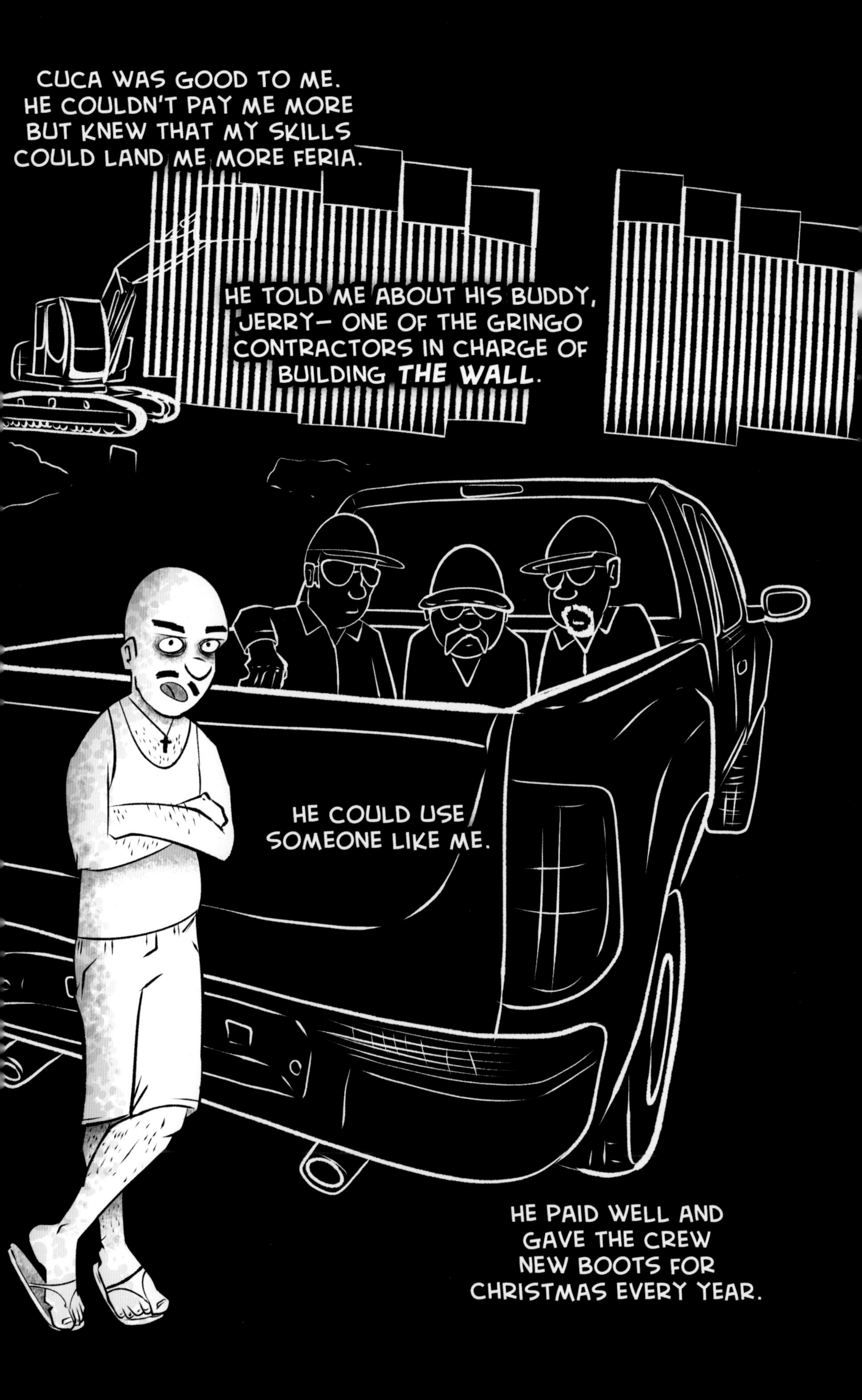
CUCA WAS GOOD TO ME. HE COULDN'T PAY ME MORE BUT KNEW THAT MY SKILLS COULD LAND ME MORE FERIA.
HE TOLD ME ABOUT HIS BUDDY, JERRY— ONE OF THE GRINGO CONTRACTORS IN CHARGE OF BUILDING **THE WALL**.
HE COULD USE SOMEONE LIKE ME.
HE PAID WELL AND GAVE THE CREW NEW BOOTS FOR CHRISTMAS EVERY YEAR.

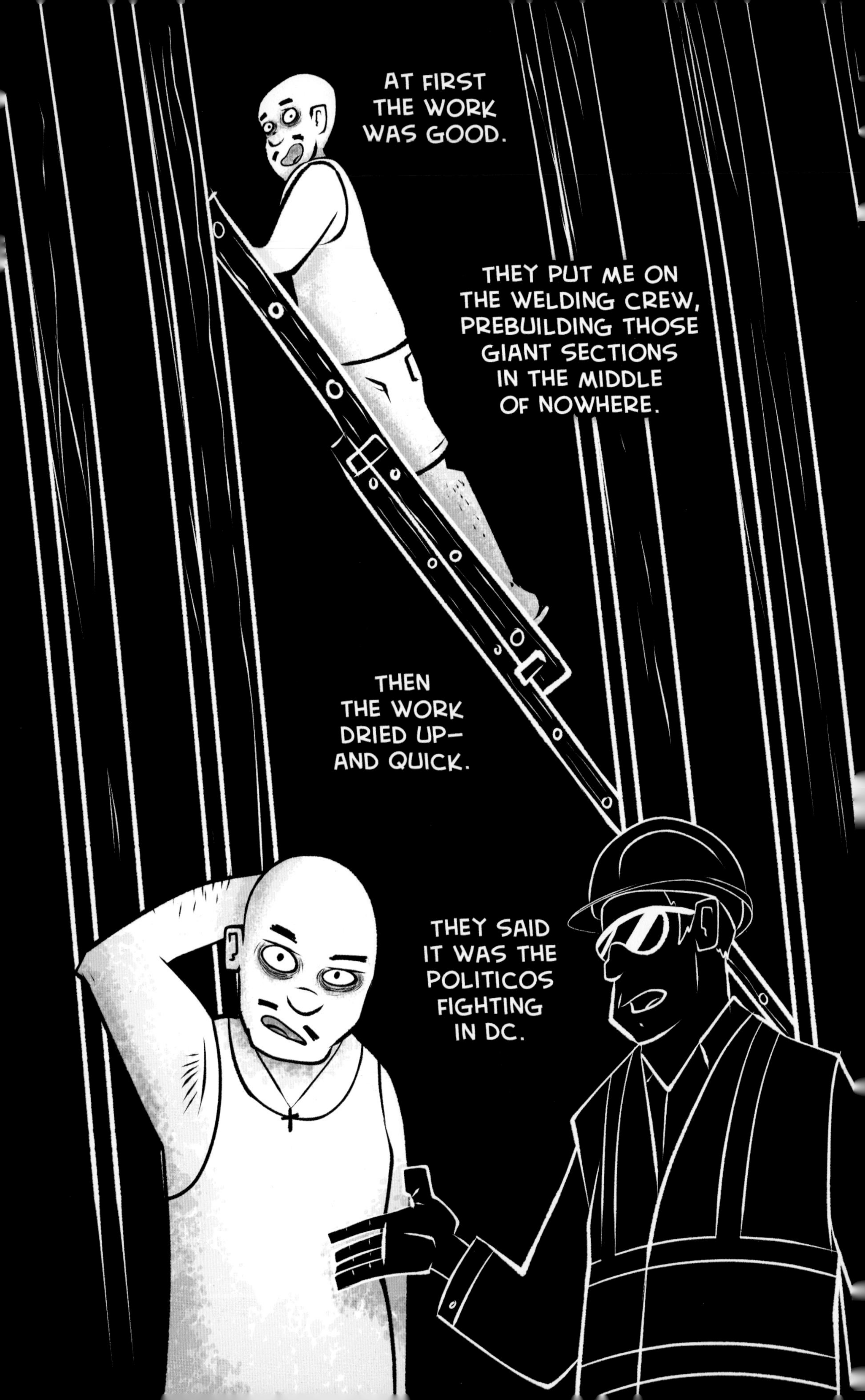
AT FIRST THE WORK WAS GOOD.
THEY PUT ME ON THE WELDING CREW, PREBUILDING THOSE GIANT SECTIONS IN THE MIDDLE OF NOWHERE.
THEN THE WORK DRIED UP— AND QUICK.
THEY SAID IT WAS THE POLITICOS FIGHTING IN DC.

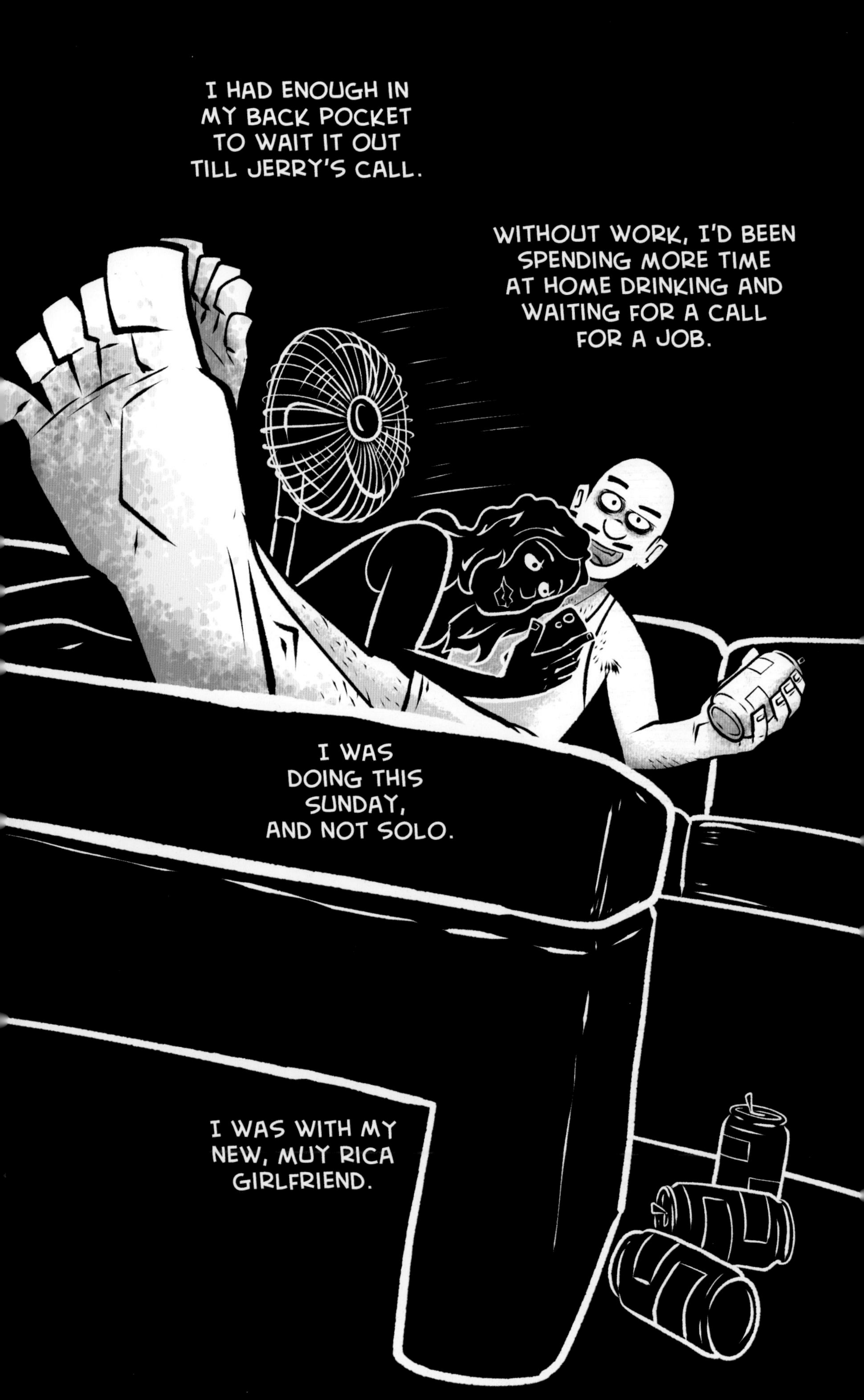
I HAD ENOUGH IN MY BACK POCKET TO WAIT IT OUT TILL JERRY'S CALL.
WITHOUT WORK, I'D BEEN SPENDING MORE TIME AT HOME DRINKING AND WAITING FOR A CALL FOR A JOB.
I WAS DOING THIS SUNDAY, AND NOT SOLO.
I WAS WITH MY NEW, MUY RICA GIRLFRIEND.

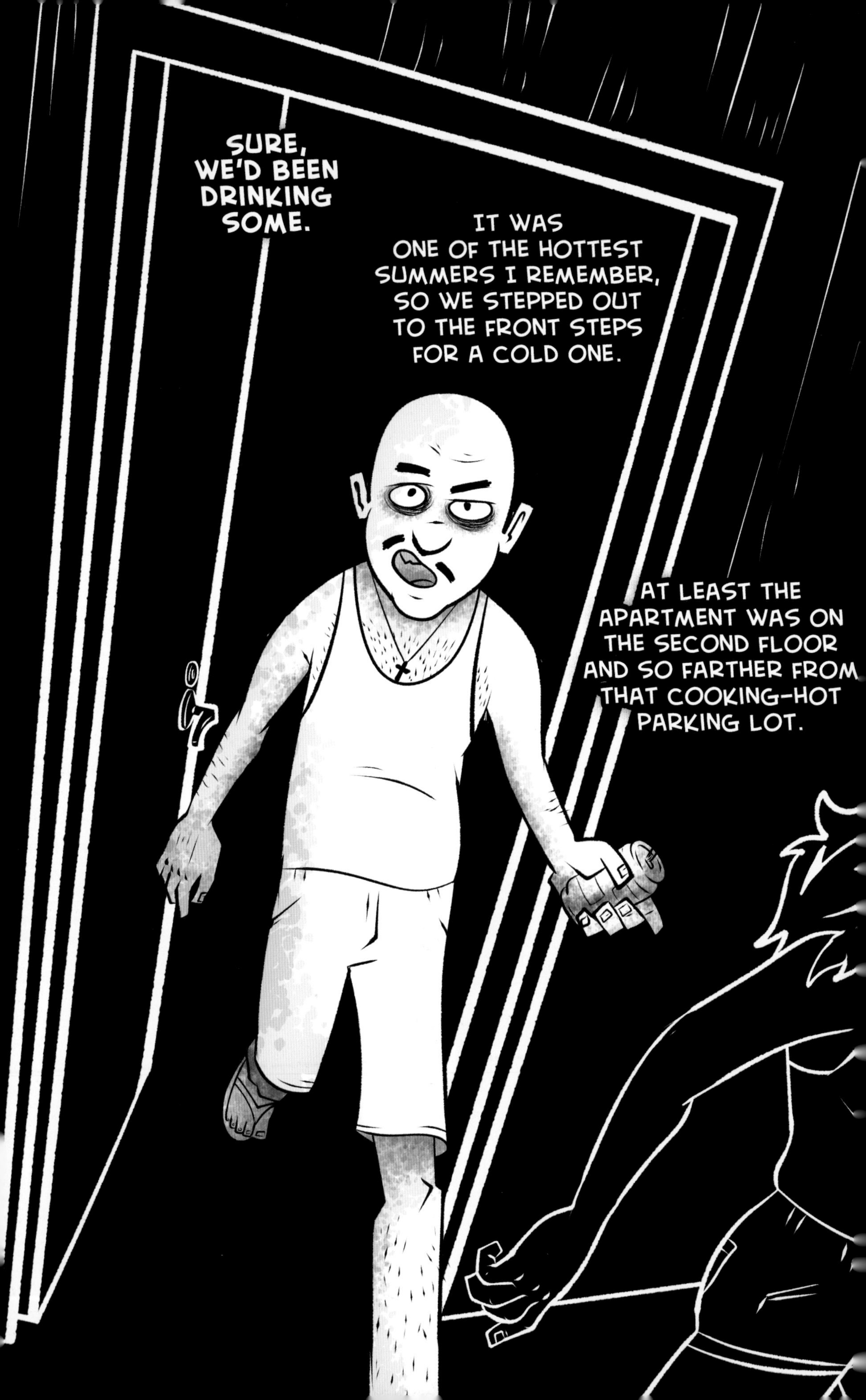
SURE, WE'D BEEN DRINKING SOME.
IT WAS ONE OF THE HOTTEST SUMMERS I REMEMBER, SO WE STEPPED OUT TO THE FRONT STEPS FOR A COLD ONE.
AT LEAST THE APARTMENT WAS ON THE SECOND FLOOR AND SO FARTHER FROM THAT COOKING-HOT PARKING LOT.

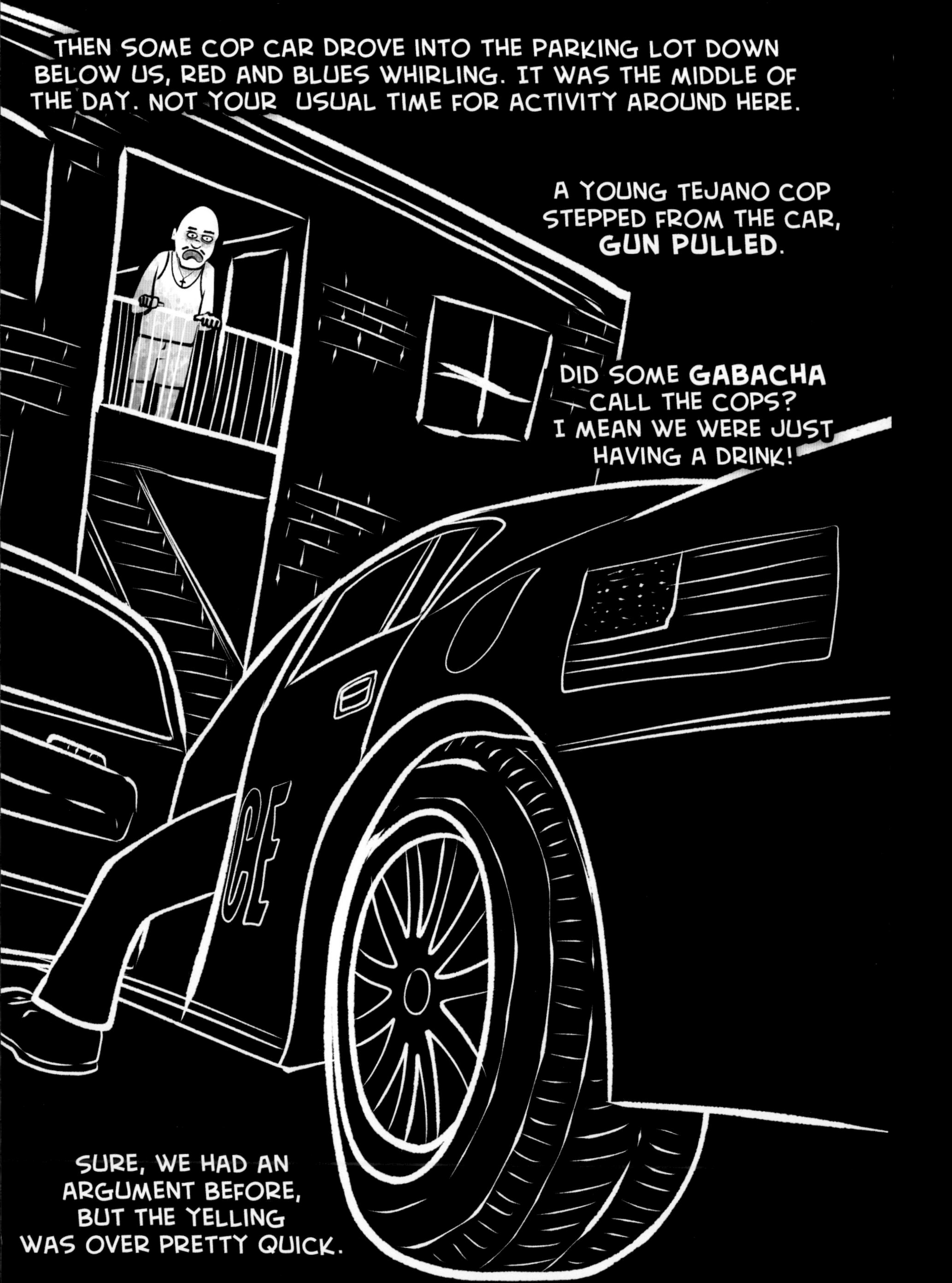
THEN SOME COP CAR DROVE INTO THE PARKING LOT DOWN BELOW US, RED AND BLUES WHIRLING. IT WAS THE MIDDLE OF THE DAY. NOT YOUR USUAL TIME FOR ACTIVITY AROUND HERE.
A YOUNG TEJANO COP STEPPED FROM THE CAR, GUN PULLED.
DID SOME GABACHA CALL THE COPS? I MEAN WE WERE JUST HAVING A DRINK!
SURE, WE HAD AN ARGUMENT BEFORE, BUT THE YELLING WAS OVER PRETTY QUICK.

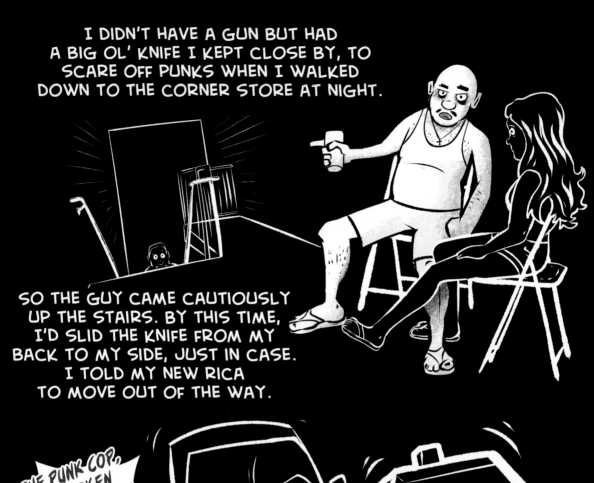

I DIDN'T HAVE A GUN BUT HAD A BIG OL' KNIFE I KEPT CLOSE BY, TO SCARE OFF PUNKS WHEN I WALKED DOWN TO THE CORNER STORE AT NIGHT.

SO THE GUY CAME CAUTIOUSLY UP THE STAIRS. BY THIS TIME, I'D SLID THE KNIFE FROM MY BACK TO MY SIDE, JUST IN CASE. I TOLD MY NEW RICA TO MOVE OUT OF THE WAY.

THE PUNK COP, IN BROKEN TEJANO SPANISH:

STEP AWAY FROM THE WOMAN!

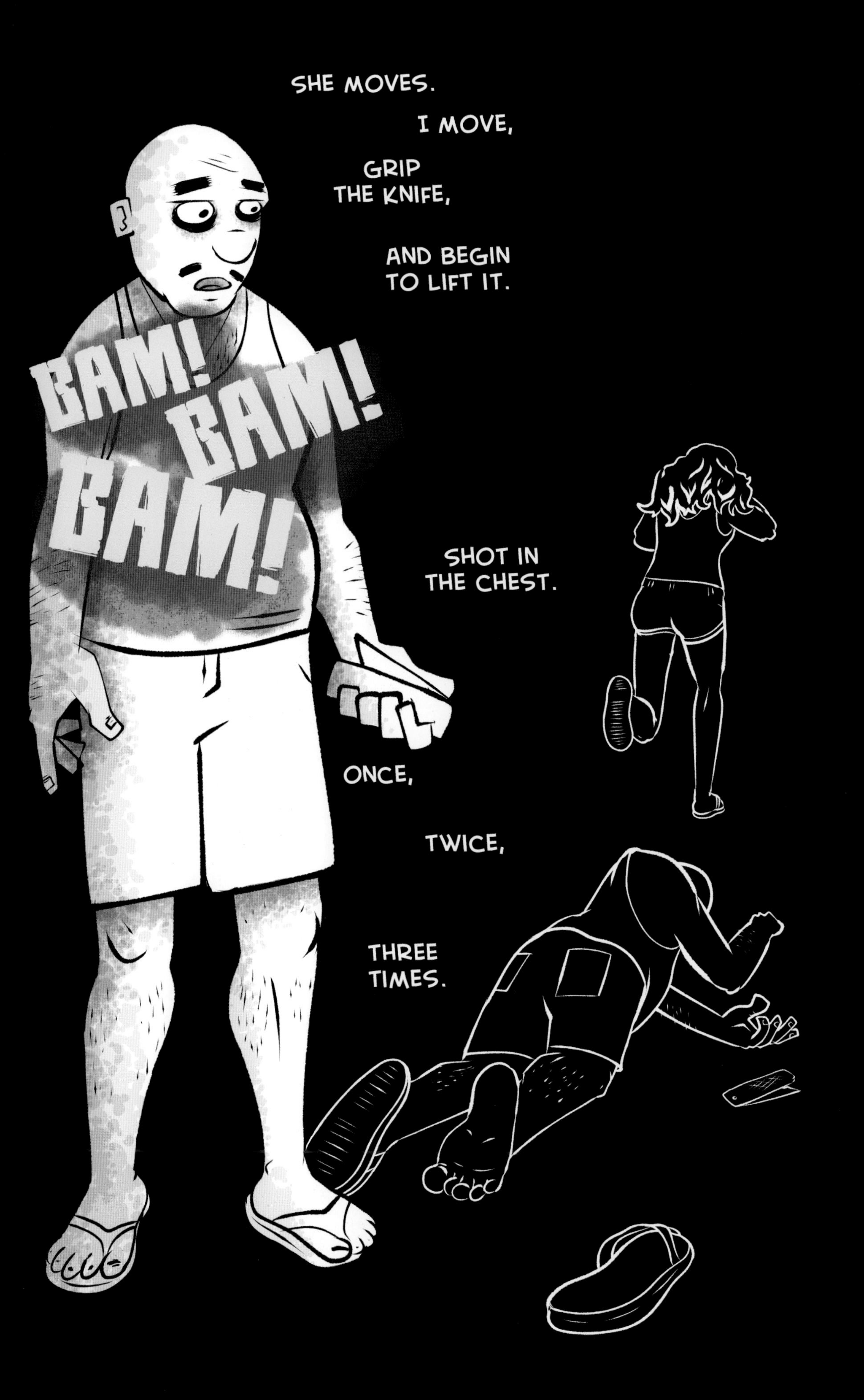
SHE MOVES.
I MOVE,
GRIP THE KNIFE,
AND BEGIN TO LIFT IT.
BAM! BAM! BAM!
SHOT IN THE CHEST.
ONCE,
TWICE,
THREE TIMES.

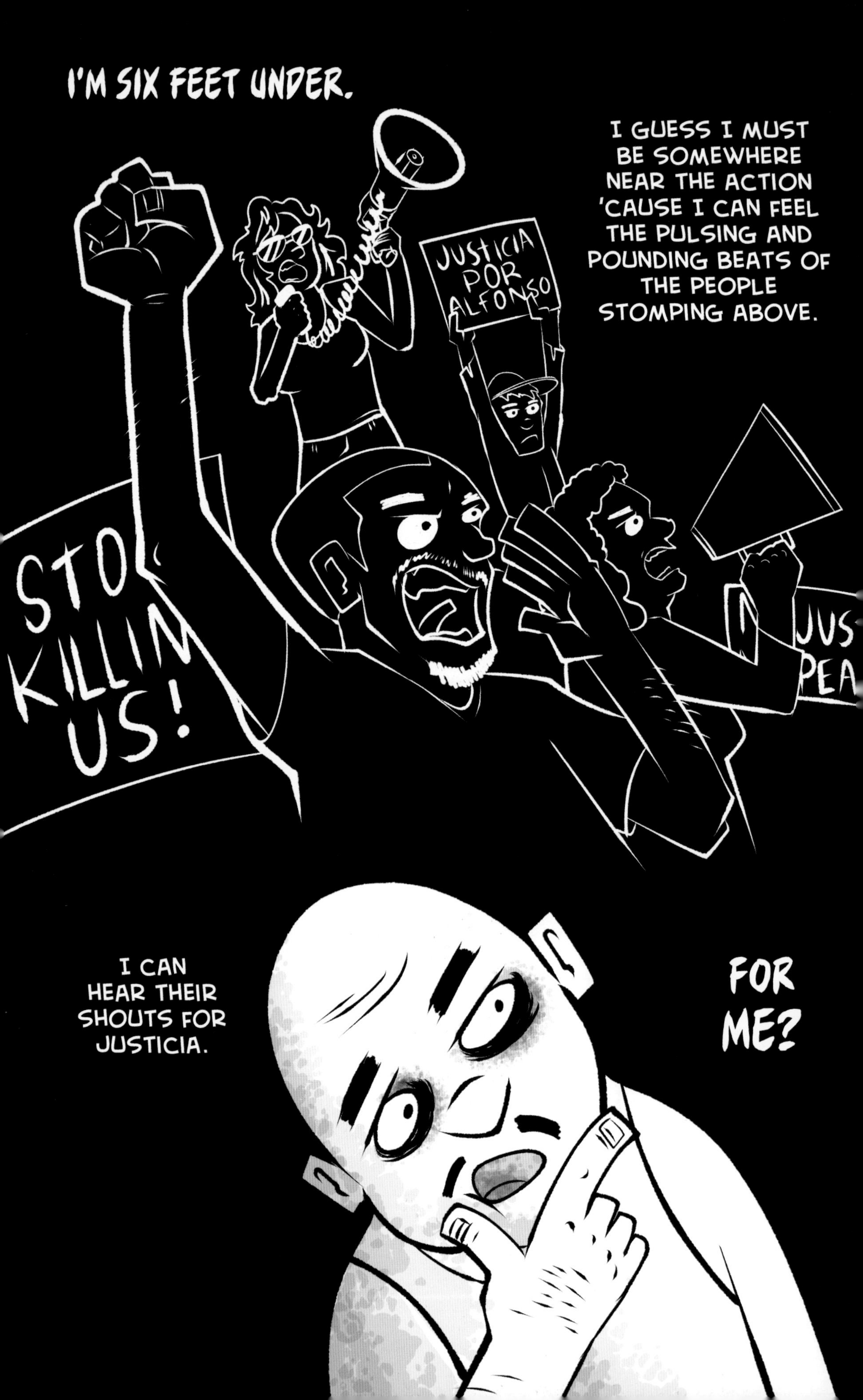
I'M SIX FEET UNDER.
I GUESS I MUST BE SOMEWHERE NEAR THE ACTION 'CAUSE I CAN FEEL THE PULSING AND POUNDING BEATS OF THE PEOPLE STOMPING ABOVE.
JUSTICIA POR ALFONSO
STO KILLIN US!
JUS PEA
I CAN HEAR THEIR SHOUTS FOR JUSTICIA.
FOR ME?

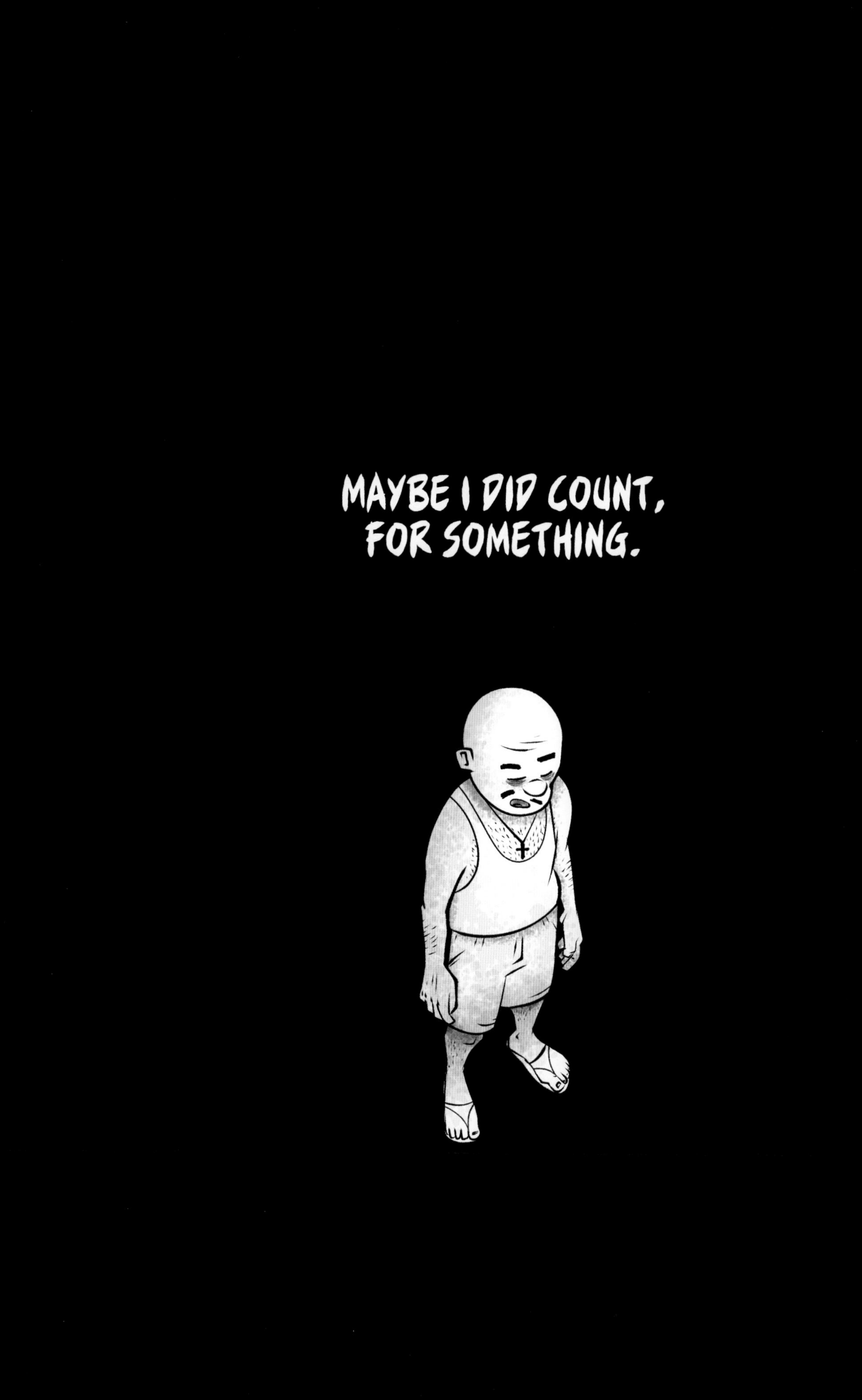
MAYBE I DID COUNT,
FOR SOMETHING.

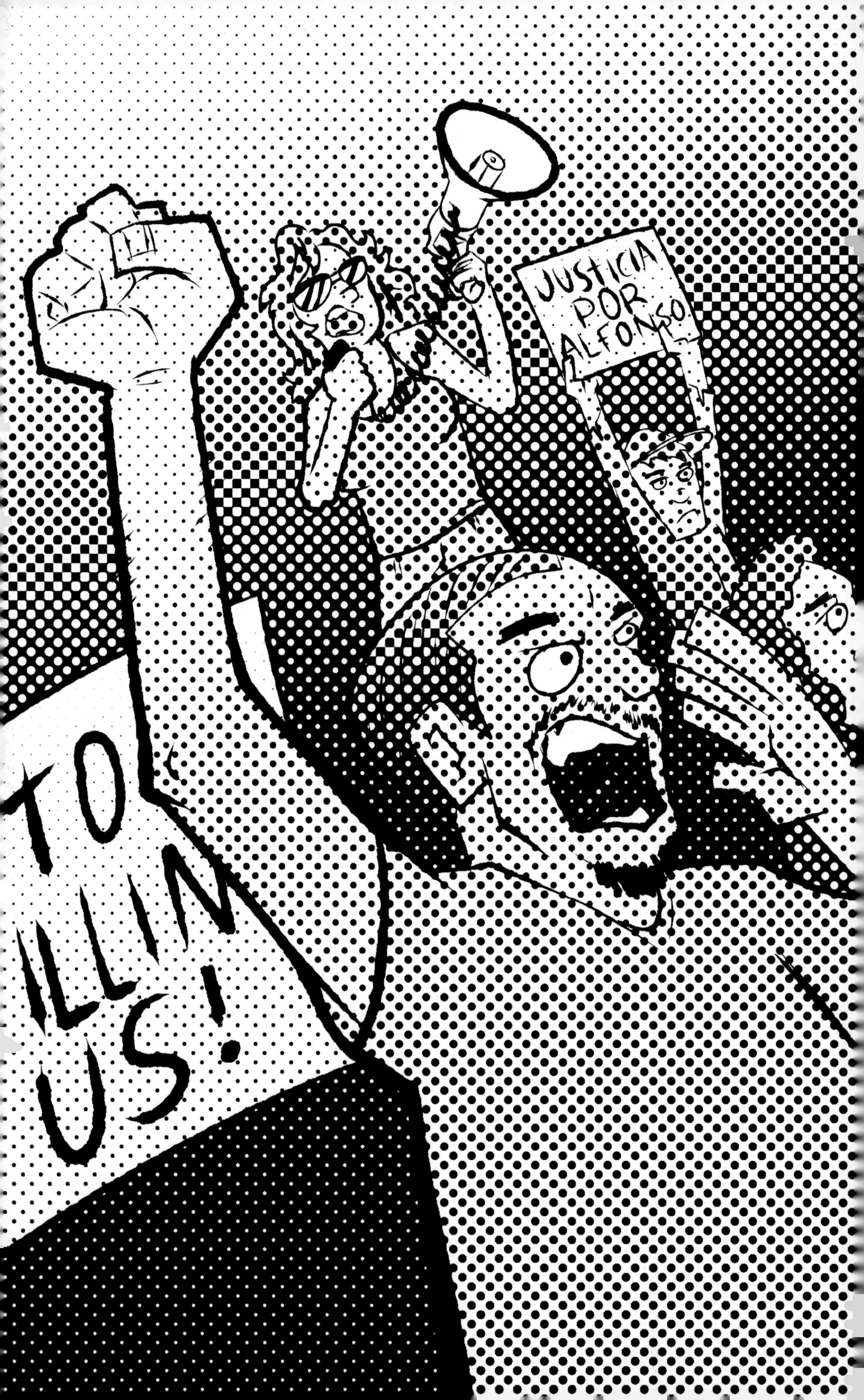
JUSTICIA POR ALFONSO
TO
ILLIN
US!

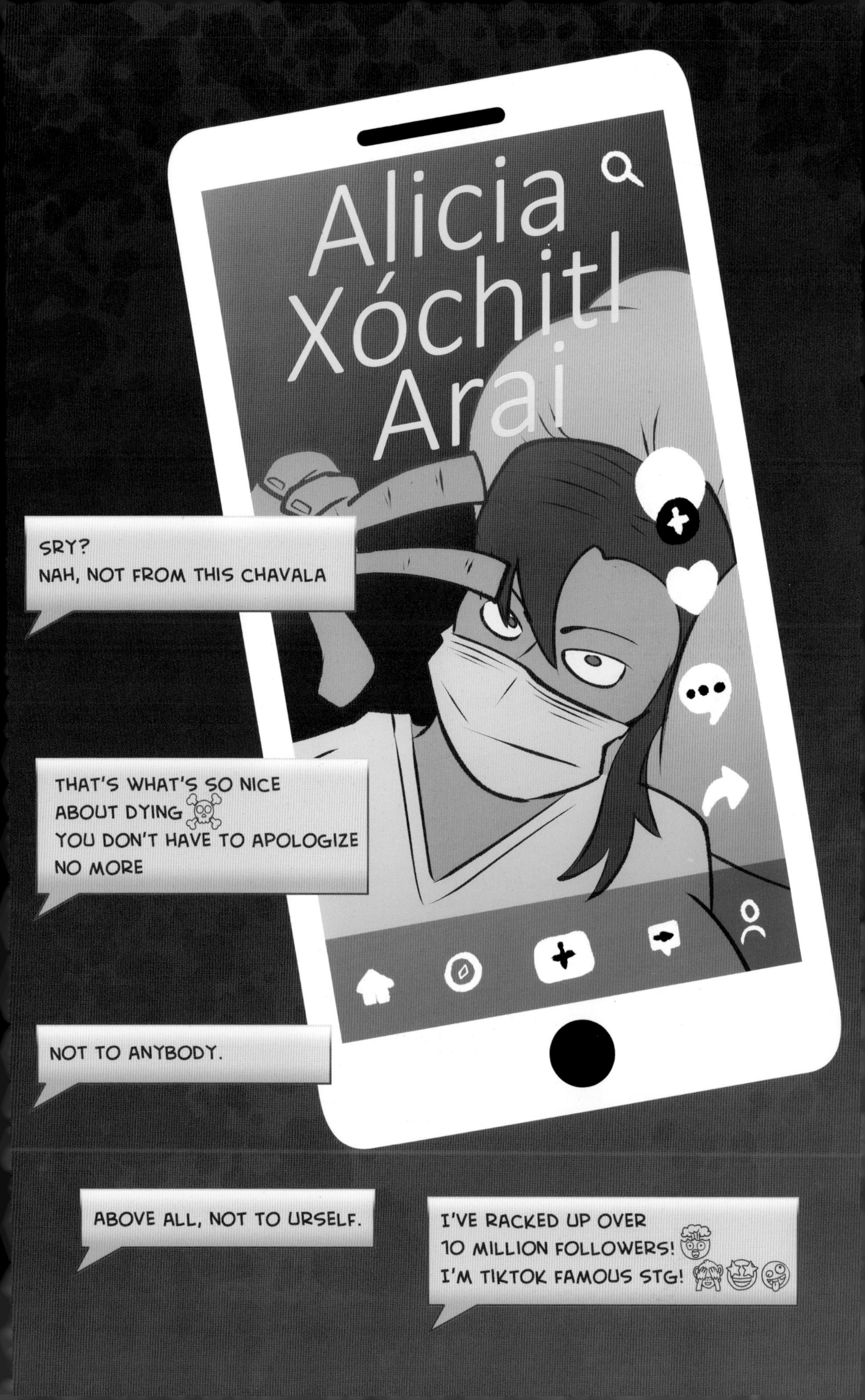
Alicia Xóchitl Arai
SRY?
NAH, NOT FROM THIS CHAVALA
THAT'S WHAT'S SO NICE
ABOUT DYING
YOU DON'T HAVE TO APOLOGIZE
NO MORE
NOT TO ANYBODY.
ABOVE ALL, NOT TO URSELF.
I'VE RACKED UP OVER
10 MILLION FOLLOWERS!
I'M TIKTOK FAMOUS STG!

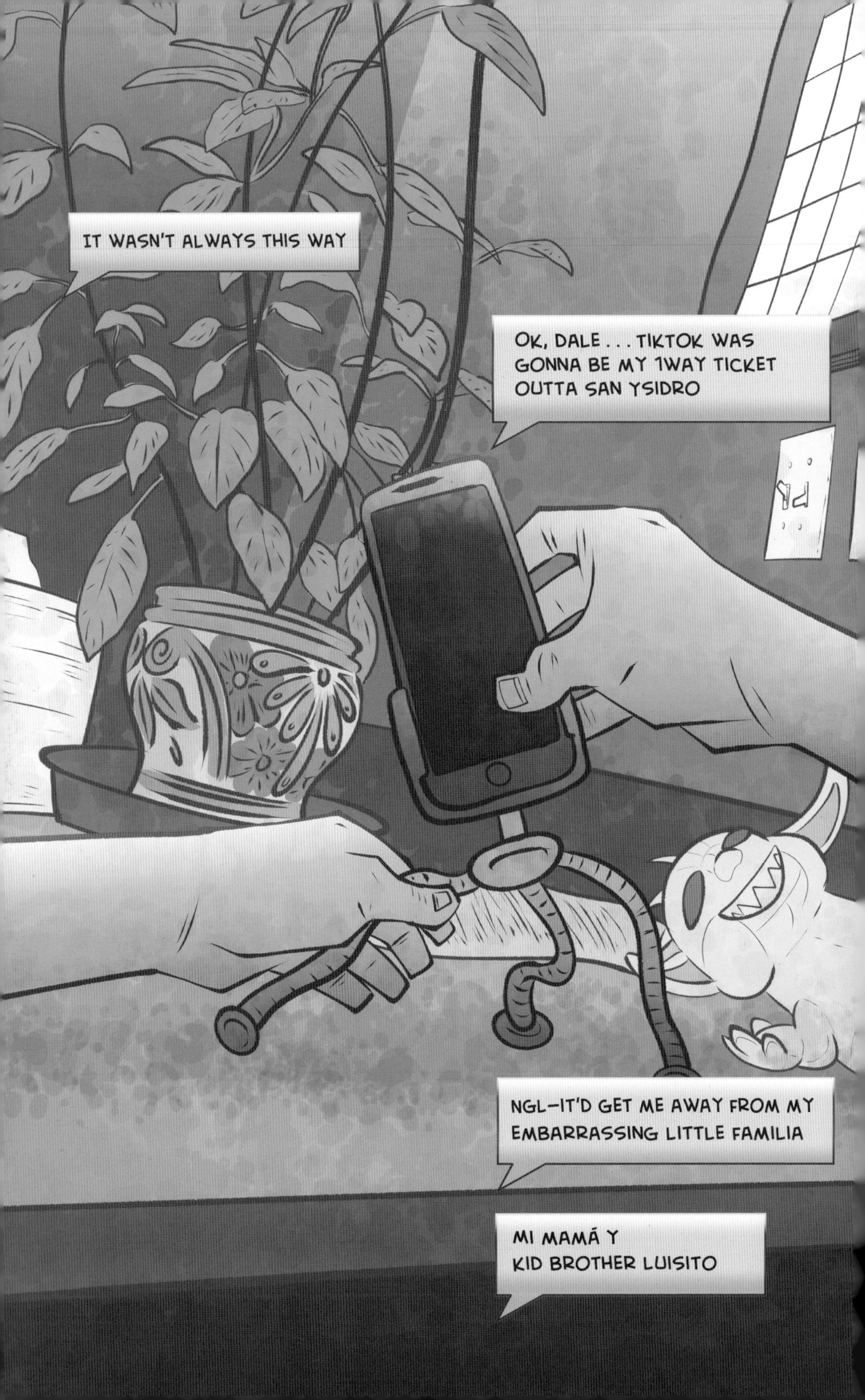
IT WASN'T ALWAYS THIS WAY
OK, DALE . . . TIKTOK WAS GONNA BE MY 1WAY TICKET OUTTA SAN YSIDRO
NGL—IT'D GET ME AWAY FROM MY EMBARRASSING LITTLE FAMILIA
MI MAMÁ Y KID BROTHER LUISITO

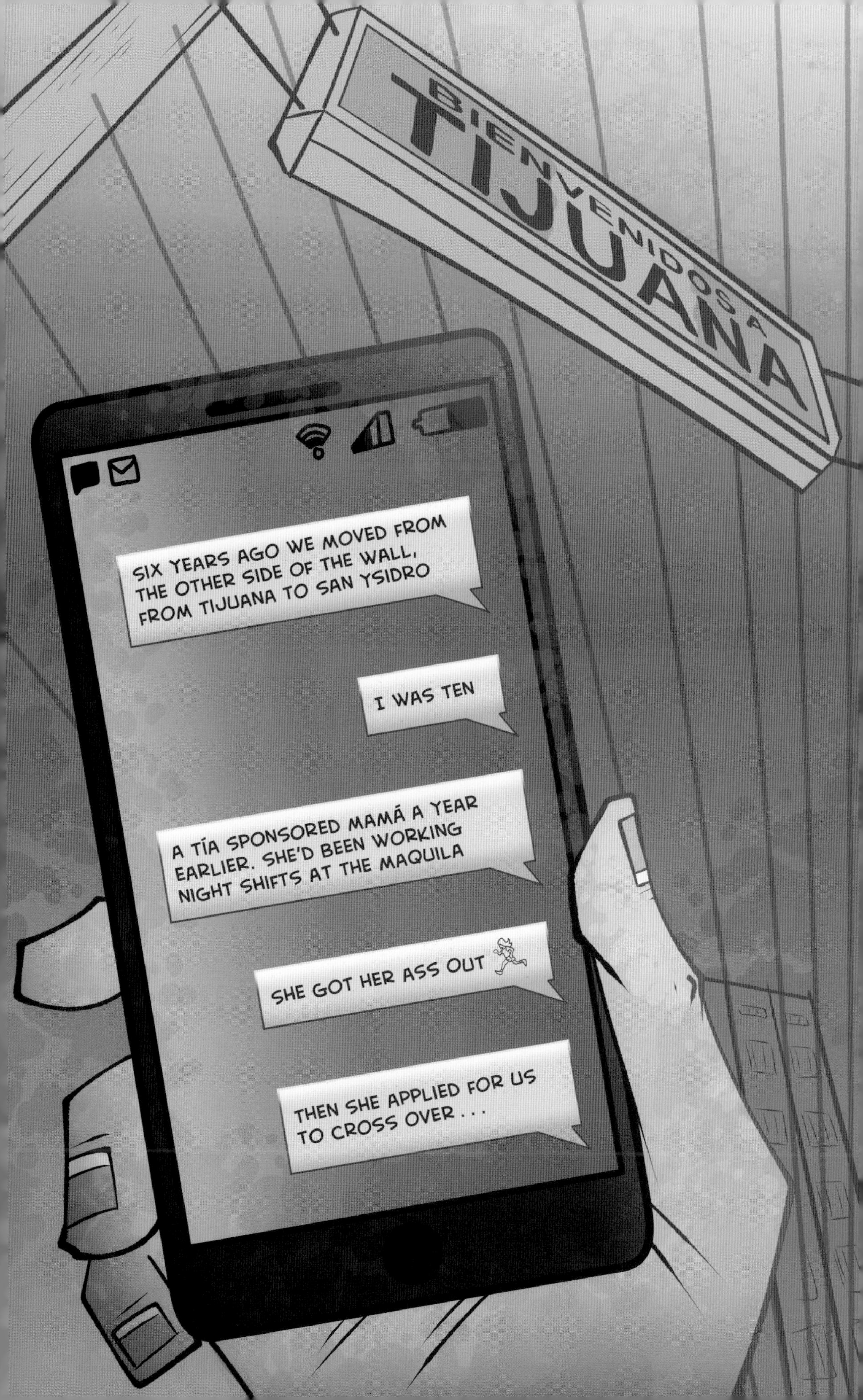
BIENVENIDOS A
TIJUANA
SIX YEARS AGO WE MOVED FROM THE OTHER SIDE OF THE WALL, FROM TIJUANA TO SAN YSIDRO
I WAS TEN
A TÍA SPONSORED MAMÁ A YEAR EARLIER. SHE'D BEEN WORKING NIGHT SHIFTS AT THE MAQUILA
SHE GOT HER ASS OUT
THEN SHE APPLIED FOR US TO CROSS OVER . . .

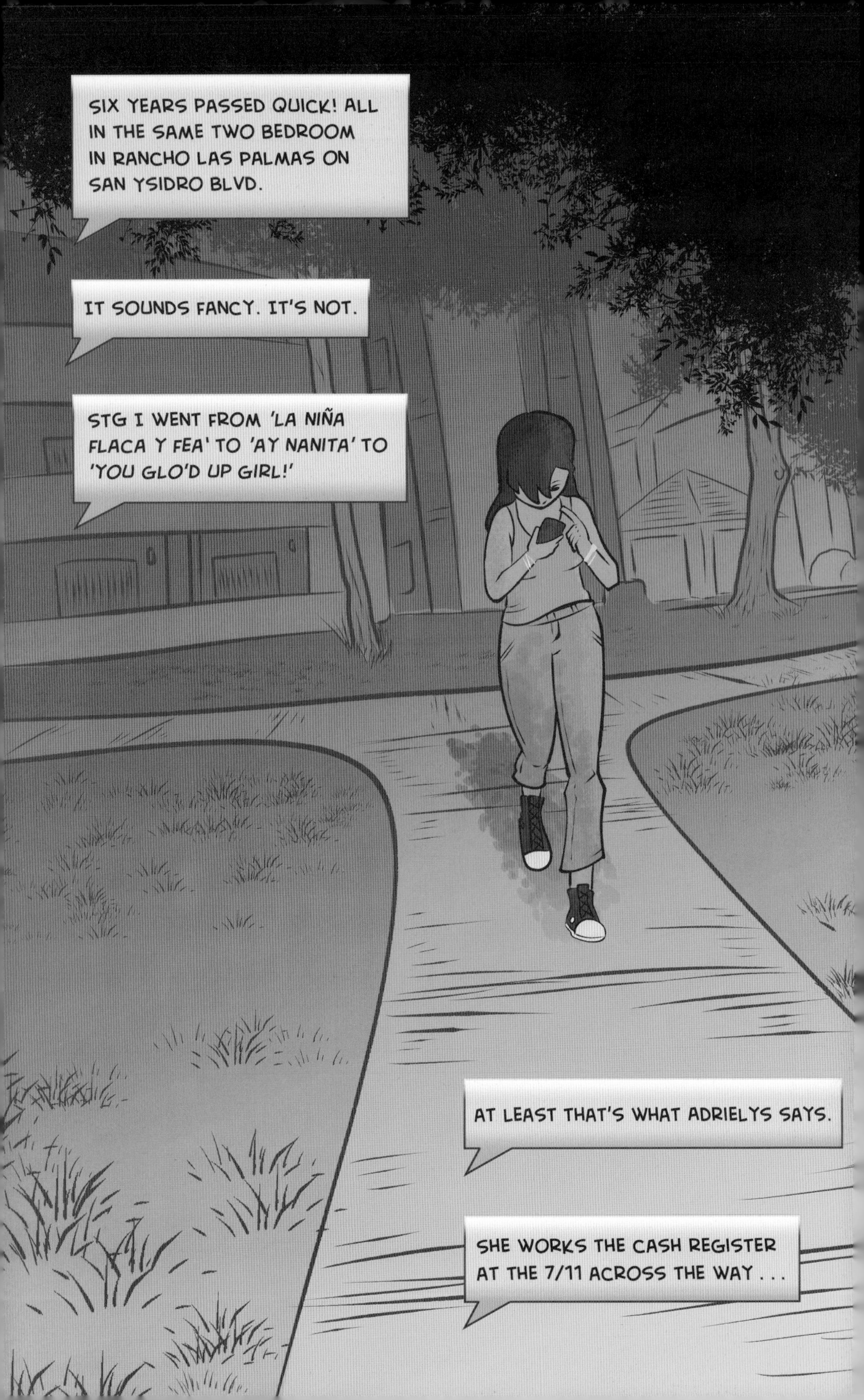
SIX YEARS PASSED QUICK! ALL IN THE SAME TWO BEDROOM IN RANCHO LAS PALMAS ON SAN YSIDRO BLVD.
IT SOUNDS FANCY. IT'S NOT.
STG I WENT FROM 'LA NIÑA FLACA Y FEA' TO 'AY NANITA' TO 'YOU GLO'D UP GIRL!'
AT LEAST THAT'S WHAT ADRIELYS SAYS.
SHE WORKS THE CASH REGISTER AT THE 7/11 ACROSS THE WAY . . .

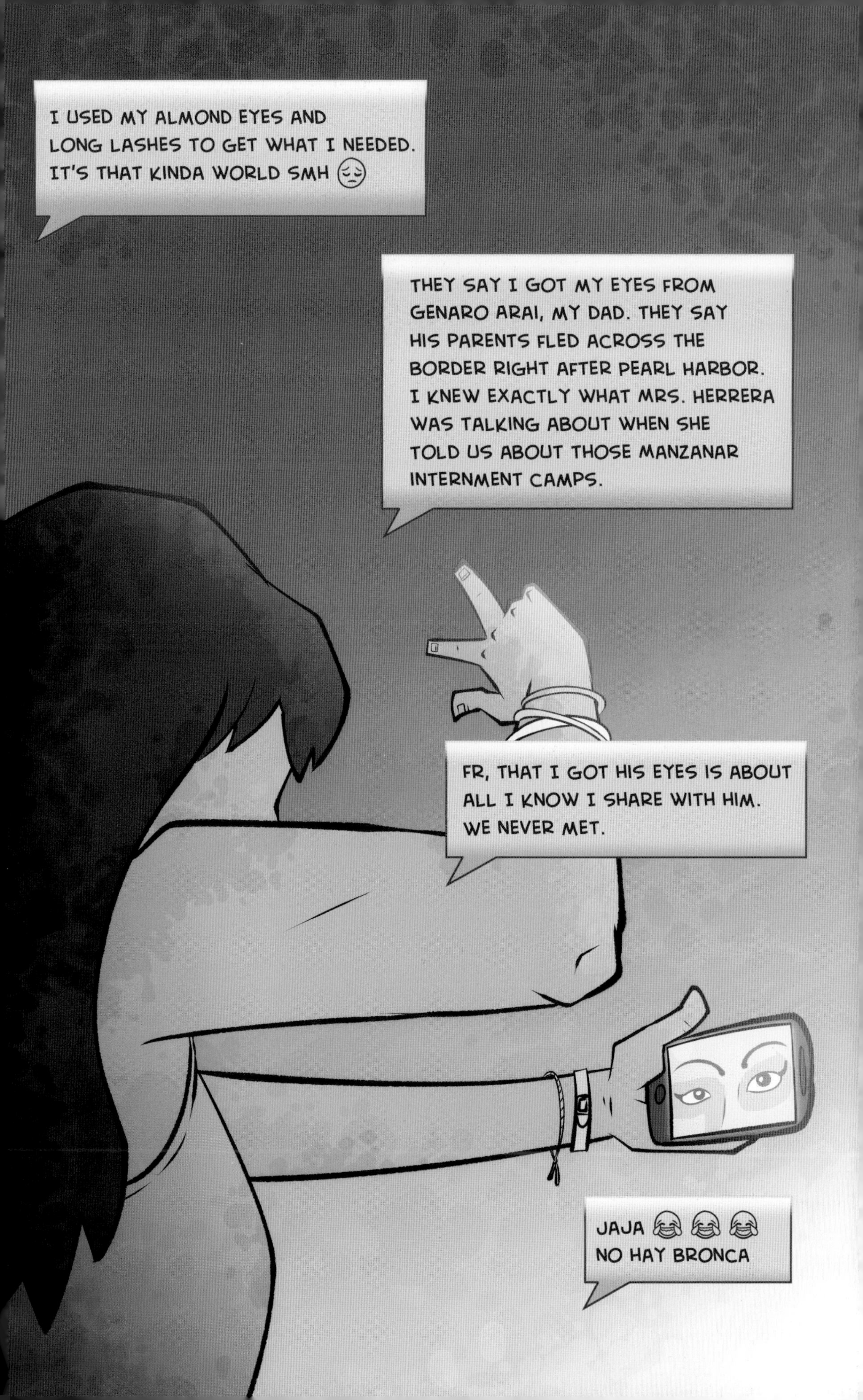
I USED MY ALMOND EYES AND LONG LASHES TO GET WHAT I NEEDED. IT'S THAT KINDA WORLD SMH
THEY SAY I GOT MY EYES FROM GENARO ARAI, MY DAD. THEY SAY HIS PARENTS FLED ACROSS THE BORDER RIGHT AFTER PEARL HARBOR. I KNEW EXACTLY WHAT MRS. HERRERA WAS TALKING ABOUT WHEN SHE TOLD US ABOUT THOSE MANZANAR INTERNMENT CAMPS.
FR, THAT I GOT HIS EYES IS ABOUT ALL I KNOW I SHARE WITH HIM. WE NEVER MET.
JAJA
NO HAY BRONCA

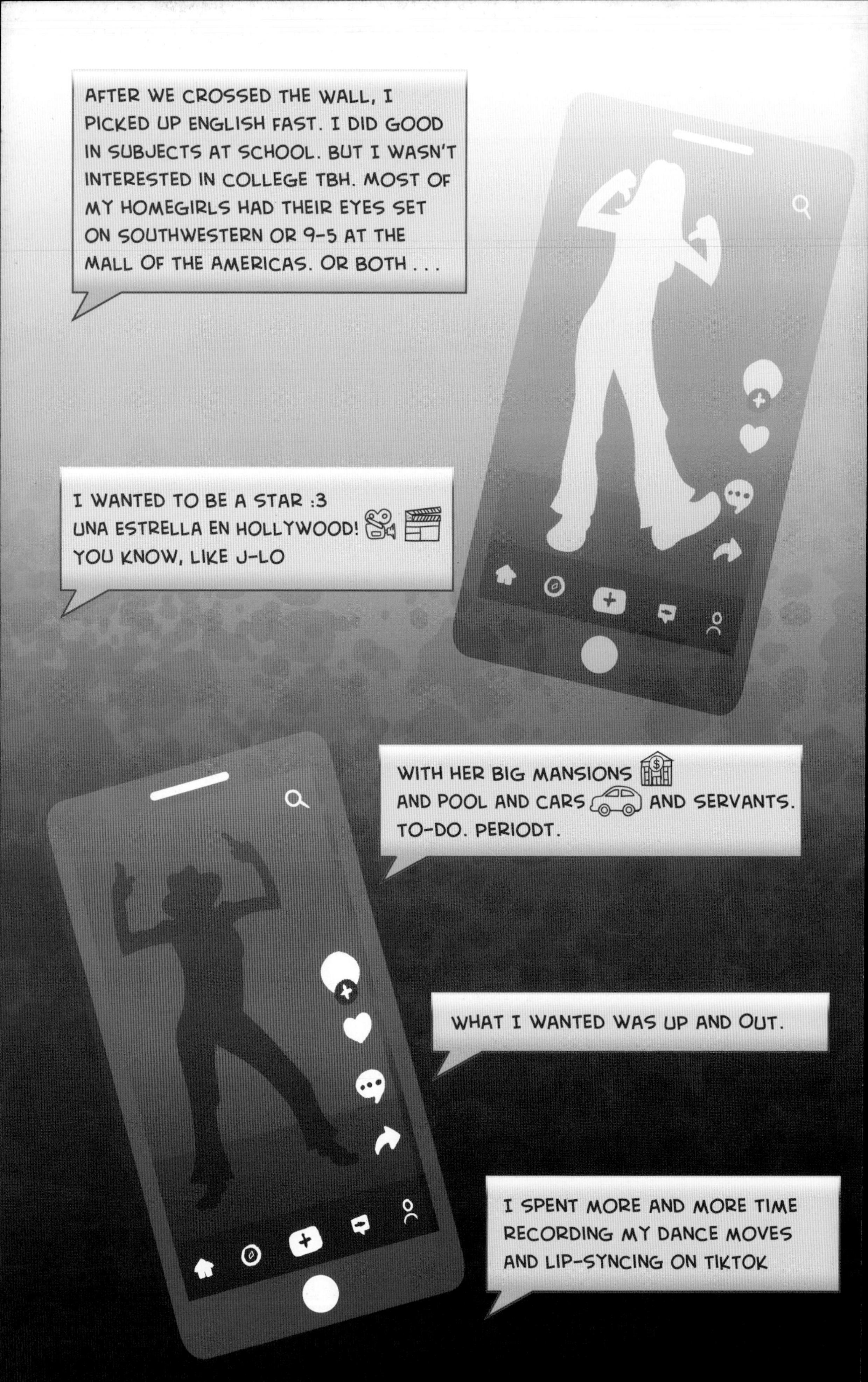
AFTER WE CROSSED THE WALL, I PICKED UP ENGLISH FAST. I DID GOOD IN SUBJECTS AT SCHOOL. BUT I WASN'T INTERESTED IN COLLEGE TBH. MOST OF MY HOMEGIRLS HAD THEIR EYES SET ON SOUTHWESTERN OR 9-5 AT THE MALL OF THE AMERICAS. OR BOTH . . .
I WANTED TO BE A STAR :3 UNA ESTRELLA EN HOLLYWOOD! YOU KNOW, LIKE J-LO
WITH HER BIG MANSIONS AND POOL AND CARS AND SERVANTS. TO-DO. PERIODT.
WHAT I WANTED WAS UP AND OUT.
I SPENT MORE AND MORE TIME RECORDING MY DANCE MOVES AND LIP-SYNCING ON TIKTOK

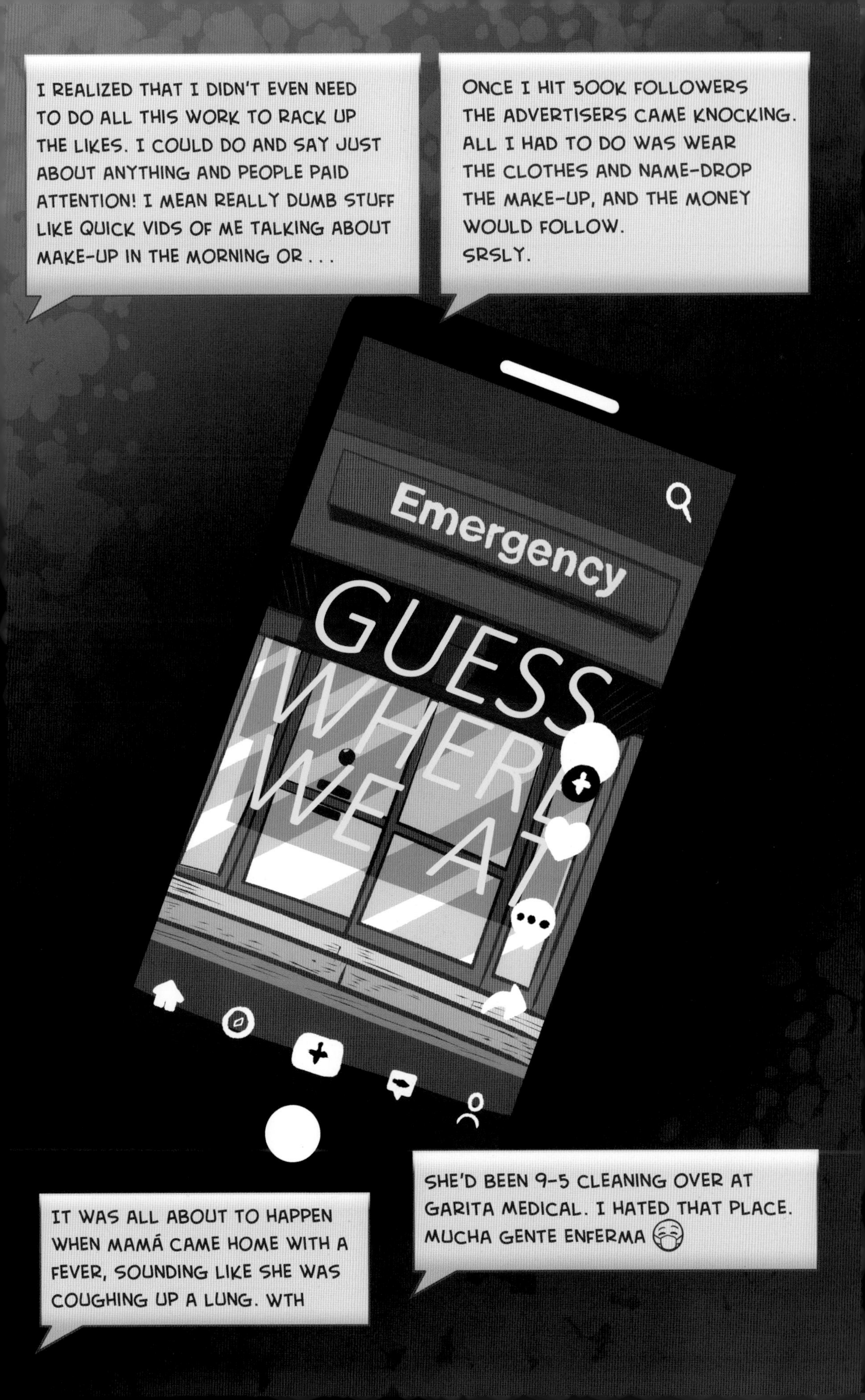
I REALIZED THAT I DIDN'T EVEN NEED TO DO ALL THIS WORK TO RACK UP THE LIKES. I COULD DO AND SAY JUST ABOUT ANYTHING AND PEOPLE PAID ATTENTION! I MEAN REALLY DUMB STUFF LIKE QUICK VIDS OF ME TALKING ABOUT MAKE-UP IN THE MORNING OR . . .
ONCE I HIT 500K FOLLOWERS THE ADVERTISERS CAME KNOCKING. ALL I HAD TO DO WAS WEAR THE CLOTHES AND NAME-DROP THE MAKE-UP, AND THE MONEY WOULD FOLLOW. SRSLY.
Emergency
GUESS WHERE WE AT
IT WAS ALL ABOUT TO HAPPEN WHEN MAMÁ CAME HOME WITH A FEVER, SOUNDING LIKE SHE WAS COUGHING UP A LUNG. WTH
SHE'D BEEN 9-5 CLEANING OVER AT GARITA MEDICAL. I HATED THAT PLACE. MUCHA GENTE ENFERMA

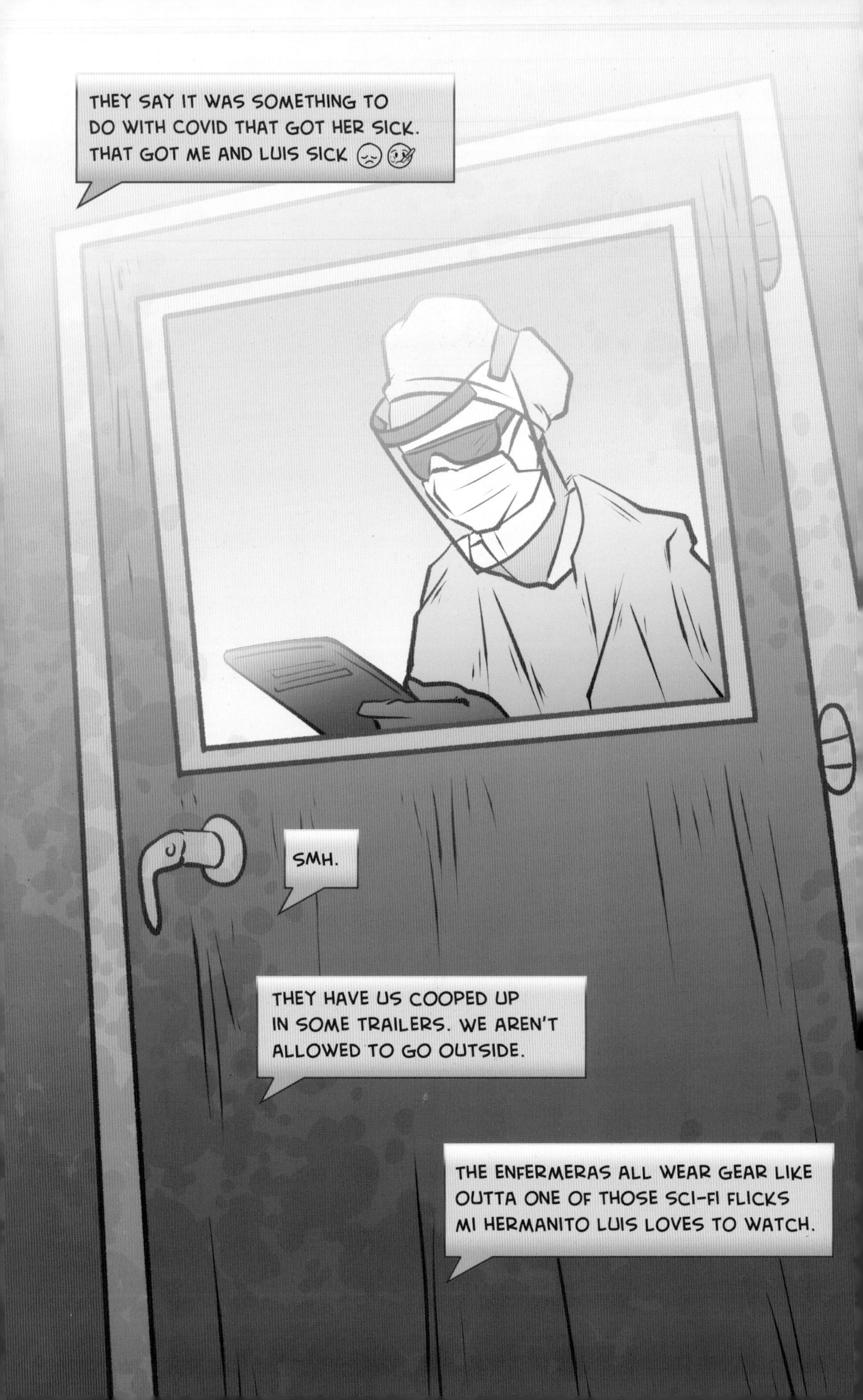
THEY SAY IT WAS SOMETHING TO DO WITH COVID THAT GOT HER SICK. THAT GOT ME AND LUIS SICK
SMH.
THEY HAVE US COOPED UP IN SOME TRAILERS. WE AREN'T ALLOWED TO GO OUTSIDE.
THE ENFERMERAS ALL WEAR GEAR LIKE OUTTA ONE OF THOSE SCI-FI FLICKS MI HERMANITO LUIS LOVES TO WATCH.

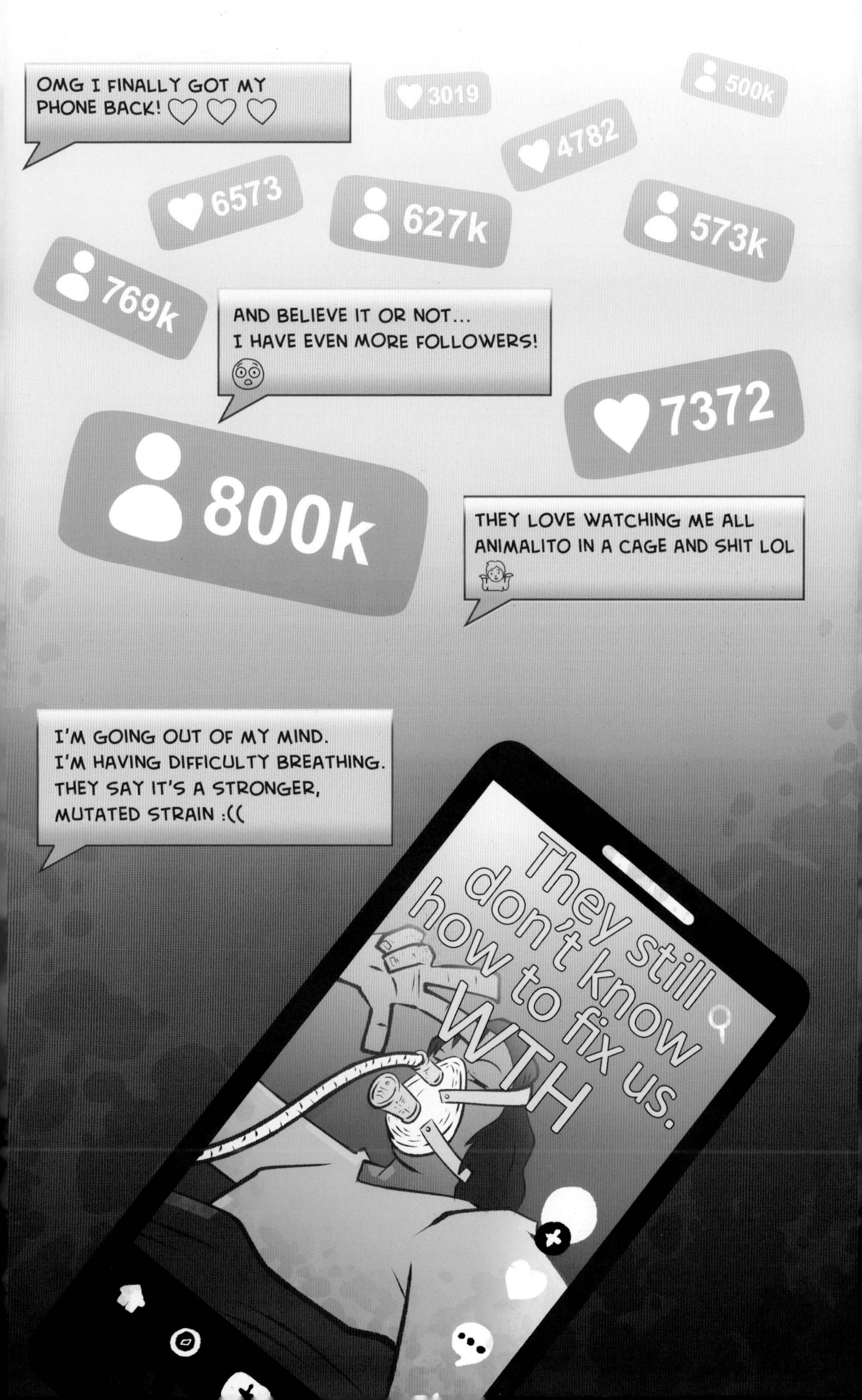
OMG I FINALLY GOT MY PHONE BACK!
3019
500k
4782
6573
627k
573k
769k
AND BELIEVE IT OR NOT... I HAVE EVEN MORE FOLLOWERS!
7372
800k
THEY LOVE WATCHING ME ALL ANIMALITO IN A CAGE AND SHIT LOL
I'M GOING OUT OF MY MIND. I'M HAVING DIFFICULTY BREATHING. THEY SAY IT'S A STRONGER, MUTATED STRAIN :((
They still don't know how to fix us. WTH

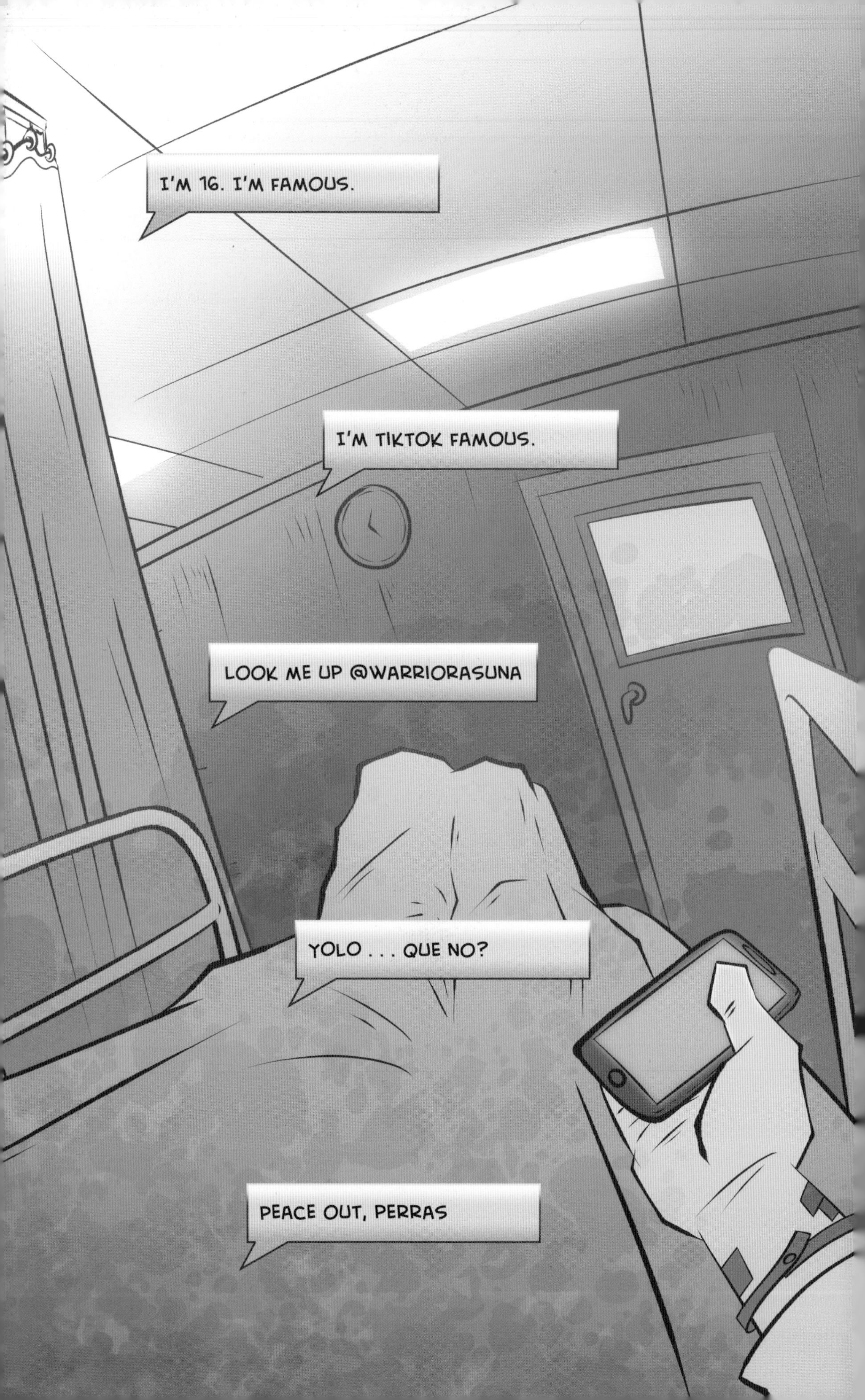
I'M 16. I'M FAMOUS.
I'M TIKTOK FAMOUS.
LOOK ME UP @WARRIORASUNA
YOLO . . . QUE NO?
PEACE OUT, PERRAS

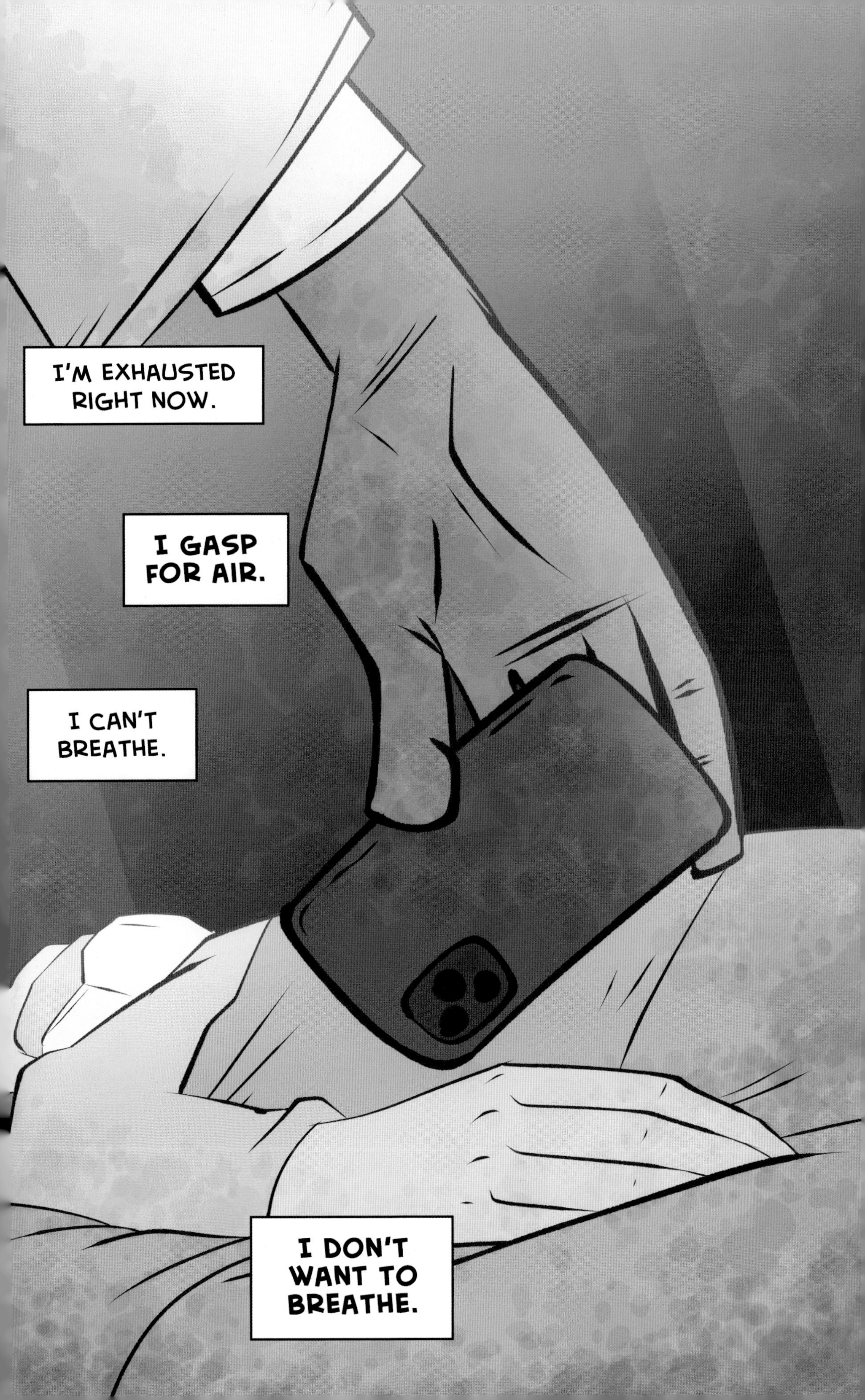
I'M EXHAUSTED RIGHT NOW.
I GASP FOR AIR.
I CAN'T BREATHE.
I DON'T WANT TO BREATHE.

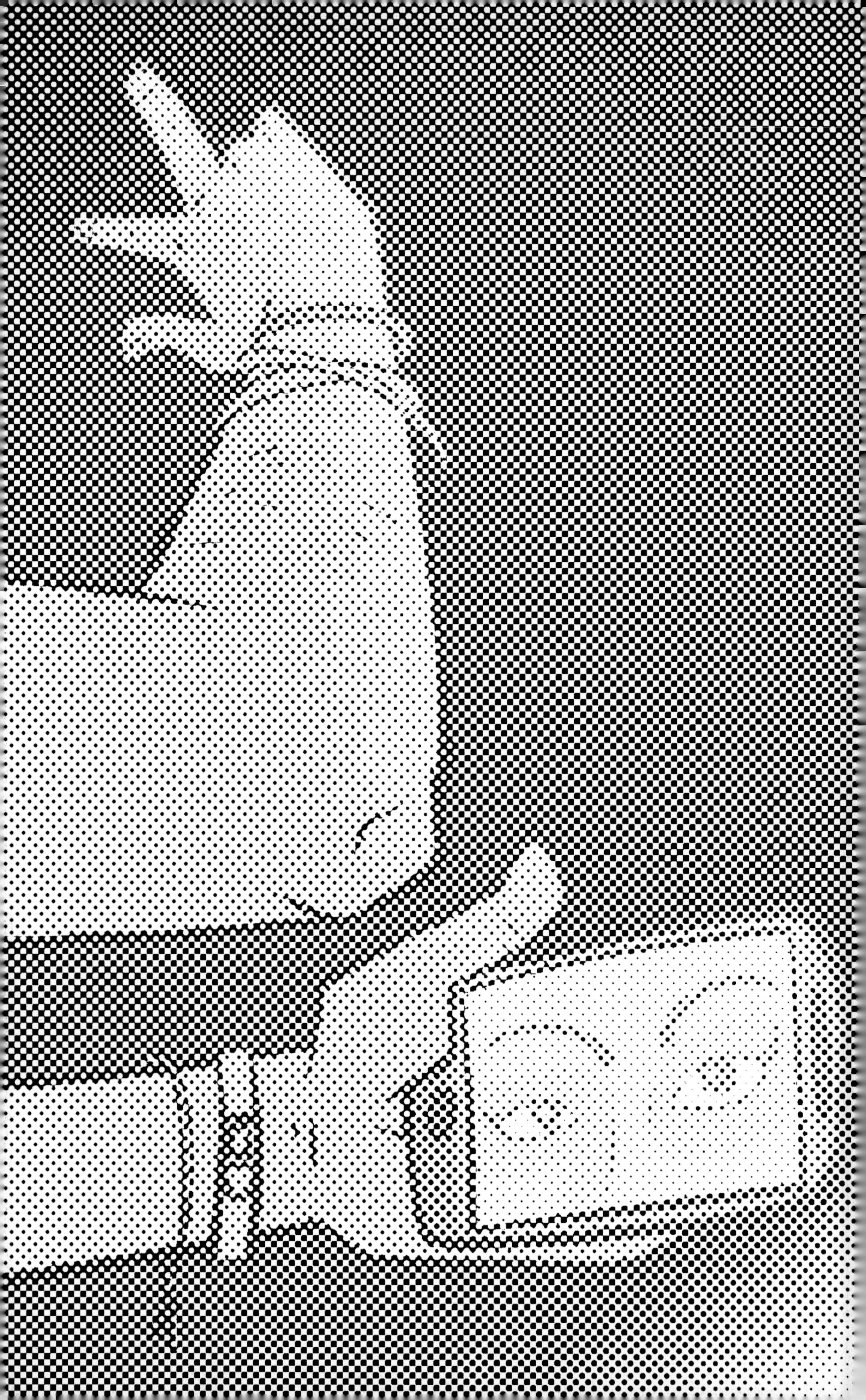

ABOUT THE AUTHOR AND
ILLUSTRATOR

FREDERICK LUIS ALDAMA is an award-winning author and editor of dozens of works of fiction, comics, animation shorts, and scholarly books, including *Tales from La Vida, The Adventures of Chupacabra Charlie,* and *Con Papá / With Papá.* The founder and director of the Latinx Pop Lab, he holds the Jacob and Frances Sanger Mossiker Chair in the Humanities at the University of Texas at Austin.

OSCAR GARZA is a comic book artist, an animator, a storyteller, and a professional comedy wrestler from Brownsville, Texas. For over two decades, he has been creating various comedy projects, including the action-comedy comic series *Mashbone & Grifty* for Chispa/Scout Comics. He lives in Austin, Texas, with his four beautiful kids.

LATINOGRAPHIX
Frederick Luis Aldama, Series Editor

This series showcases trade graphic and comic books—graphic novels, memoir, nonfiction, and more—by Latinx writers and artists. The series aims to be rich and complex, bringing on projects with any balance of text and visual narrative, from larger graphic narratives to collections of vignettes or serial comics, in color and black and white, both fiction and non-fiction. Projects in the series take up themes of all kinds, exploring topics from immigration to family, education to identity. The series provides a place for exploration and boundary pushing and celebrates hybridity, experimentation, and creativity. Projects are produced with quality and care and exemplify the full breadth of creative visual work being created by today's Latinx artists.

Through Fences
WRITTEN BY FREDERICK LUIS ALDAMA
ILLUSTRATED BY OSCAR GARZA

Con Papá / With Papá
WRITTEN BY FREDERICK LUIS ALDAMA
ILLUSTRATED BY NICKY RODRIGUEZ

Las aventuras de Chupacabra Charlie
FREDERICK LUIS ALDAMA
ILUSTRADO POR CHRIS ESCOBAR

United States of Banana: A Graphic Novel
GIANNINA BRASCHI AND JOAKIM LINDENGREN
EDITED AND WITH AN INTRODUCTION BY AMANDA M. SMITH AND AMY SHEERAN

The Adventures of Chupacabra Charlie
WRITTEN BY FREDERICK LUIS ALDAMA
ILLUSTRATED BY CHRIS ESCOBAR

Thunderbolt: An American Tale, Vol. 1
WILFRED SANTIAGO

Tales from la Vida: A Latinx Comics Anthology
EDITED BY FREDERICK LUIS ALDAMA

Drawing on Anger: Portraits of U.S. Hypocrisy
ERIC J. GARCÍA

Angelitos: A Graphic Novel
ILAN STAVANS AND SANTIAGO COHEN

Diary of a Reluctant Dreamer: Undocumented Vignettes from a Pre-American Life
ALBERTO LEDESMA